REITERATIONS

ALSO BY DAVID ARMSTRONG

Going Anywhere: Stories

REITERATIONS

stories by

DAVID ARMSTRONG

newamericanpress

Milwaukee, Wis.

newamericanpress

www.NewAmericanPress.com

Printed in the United States of America

ISBN 978-1-941561-05-8

Book design by David Bowen

Cover image © Igor Cheri

For ordering information, please contact:

Ingram Book Group
One Ingram Blvd.
La Vergne, TN 37086
(800) 937-8000
orders@ingrambook.com

For Allan

TABLE OF CONTENTS

I.

In which is discussed the violence of men
and the strength of women.

1st Iteration   LOST-AND-FOUND GIRLS   11

2nd Iteration   FRENCH FOR WEAKLING   29

II.

In which is discussed disenfranchisement and alienation.

1st Iteration   EGGS AND BACON AND COFFEE   53

2nd Iteration   TRUTH BE TOLD   67

III.

In which is discussed the remnants of a marriage.

1st Iteration   KAPOK   77

2nd Iteration   I THOUGHT OF YOU   97

IV.

In which the word is made manifest.

1st Iteration   ESCAPE   117

2nd Iteration   LEADS   129

V.

In which a primate appears.

1st Iteration   FIERCEST TRAITS   133

2nd Iteration   GRACILE   155

VI.

In which a father is sought.

1st Iteration   TRACKING   177

2nd Iteration   DEPARTURES AND ARRIVALS   179

Acknowledgments   187

About the Writer   189

REPETITION.

It is an excellent thing to express a thing
consecutively in two ways, and thus provide it
with a right and a left foot. Truth can stand
indeed on one leg, but with two she will walk
and complete her journey.

— Friedrich Nietzsche, *Human, All Too Human*

LOST-AND-FOUND GIRLS

1. **Jolynn Sweeney. Age: 23. Lemmon, SD. 1967.**
   *At the center of town is a minor tourist attraction
   Petrified Wood Park, a collection of rock piles resembling the
   cairns of an ancient people. What looks like the mausoleum
   of a Viking king sits in the center, the black maw of its
   entrance waiting. Three blocks away, at the town's edge, sits
   the Rushmore Motor Lodge, a desolate little scab of a
   building with cinderblock walls and windows yellowed by
   cigarette smoke. In such a place they find her, moldering.
   The liquids leak from her body in such a way as to make it
   appear as if she is weeping black tears.*

SEVERAL ACCOUNTS, EASILY CONFIRMED, EXIST OF BODIES BEING discovered beneath mattresses in hotel rooms. Once you start looking, the stories are everywhere. Usually a result of the smell, the remains are stumbled upon by maids, attendants, managers and, of course, the occasional guest. The most horrific, chill-inducing tales are those in which the lodgers have stayed one or many nights sleeping comfortably eight inches above a rotting corpse.

Heath Plunkett thought about this as he exited the Venetian Hotel into the late afternoon heat of Las Vegas with his wife, Shannon, but he didn't express it. This is what he was thinking. Girls beneath mattresses. Story upon story. Jessica Pontain. He hadn't told Shannon the real reason he'd agreed to come, and he certainly hadn't told her about the envelope tucked away inside his jacket.

"People say how Las Vegas is a seedy place," Shannon said, "but I think it's beautiful." He could hear her voice trying to lift off, to separate her from the distress that had descended upon them in the past two years. She was forty-three but lately had succumbed to a deeper aging. Heath saw the same wear on his own face in the mirror in the mornings.

Shannon pointed to the Bellagio fountains like an explorer. "Every fifteen minutes. A different song, a different choreography."

Standing before the spray's overwhelming whoosh, he felt a slight sense of giddiness. A recording of Lee Greenwood singing "God Bless the USA" filled him with possibility, even hope. If only he could get away from Shannon.

For the next two hours they traversed the Strip, skirting drunks and maneuvering around the big groups of tourists taking pictures of the half-size Eiffel Tower. They saw the monstrous MGM lion, the eerie jesters of carnivale holding court above Harrah's entrance, the obelisk-like facade of the Cosmopolitan and the whole assault of oversized Harleys, M&Ms, guitars, showgirls, cabarets, and acrobats calling to crowds from signs overhead.

Near the intersection of Flamingo, a short man with what looked like a stack of baseball cards flipped them against his thigh, giving off the bright shuffling sound that cards make when wedged into the spokes of a bicycle. The man held them out to Heath, and instinctively Heath took them as he passed. Staring down he saw a nude woman and for a moment mistook it for a playing card like the ones his roommate had used to deal poker in college. He still remembered the over-glammed look of those women on the playing cards, their teased and hairsprayed bangs pushed up to peacock heights, their backs arched ridiculously so their breasts pointed to the heavens, their open, soft legs slightly turned to reveal the trimmed pubic hair but not what was beneath. The picture on the card was not that different, suggestive in the least subtle ways, the hairstyles equally outdated somehow. But these weren't playing cards. They were advertisements for girls. You could call. They'd come to your room. The rates were cheap. Thirty-five, forty dollars.

Shannon looked down at the cards.

"I didn't know that's what I was being handed," he said.

"You never know what hand you're going to be dealt," she said.

He searched for a trash can, found none, and jammed the cards deep into his pocket.

They returned to the hotel, and he couldn't sleep. After an hour of staring blankly at the ceiling, he arose, dressed silently, checked for the cards in his pocket, and descended to the Strip. The crowds had multiplied. Waves of boozy twenty-somethings rolled by, whole masses of swaying bodies and laughter. Heath pulled out the cards and selected the woman with the darkest hair.

He stared for a very long time at his phone before dialing the number.

2. **Eliza Fishbeck. Age: 47. Socorro County, NM. 2004.**
    Off a stretch of State Route 439 on a road called Otero
    sits an unlikely bed and breakfast called the Spouter Inn—
    the old owner was a Cape Cod native. There is no
    quaintness to the place. Bleak cornfields scratch at the gravel
    and dilapidated asphalt. Junked tractor parts and old
    McDonald's wrappers litter the ditches. Here they find Eliza
    Fishbeck beneath the mattress in her room three weeks after
    her ex-husband, from whom she'd been running, tracked her
    down. The owners are elderly and heard nothing. Never once
    during that three weeks did they enter Eliza's room, which
    had a DO NOT DISTURB sign hanging from the doorknob.
    When asked by a reporter why they waited so long, the
    couple replied that they didn't want to bother Eliza for fear
    she might write a bad review on one of those internet sites
    they heard about.

She was not at all what he'd ordered. Not even close to the age of the girl on the card. She was stringy, with ropy veins bulging in her hands like she worked out too often. Her hair was a mucked-up blonde, and her breasts had been hiked up by a complicated dress and underwire so they looked like pieces of a parade float losing their shape in the rain. She met him near a lounge at the back of the Paris casino, under the brilliant blue sky painted on the ceiling. Maybe not the girl from the card, but he could still tell it was the woman sent to meet him. She had a bored way of shambling through tourists. She wore cheap shoes made to look expensive. Her lipstick was like a lacquer, like fake lips on an unmoving mouth.

She knew him, too. By the way he was standing, he guessed. Waiting for someone.

He handed her the forty dollars, then a hundred. He knew that must be next, to get her to stay. He was familiar with sales. He'd written copy in his early days for businesses taking out ads with the newspaper where he worked. One rule was, you never put the final price on the ad. The 'get-em-in-the-door-price,' that's what his first boss called it. Get the deal going. Then pile on the rest. The woman rubbed her thumb over Ben Franklin's face as if this were her special way of checking for fake currency.

"Jezzabelle," she said. "Two Zs."

"Harold," Heath said.

She smiled. "Yeah, okay, Harold. Where to?"

"Golden Sunset Motor Court," he said.

"You're not staying here?"

"No. I'm off the Strip."

She hesitated, but the pause was brief. "It'll cost you," she said. He handed her another hundred. He didn't know what the normal prices were, but he didn't want to negotiate. It only mattered that she come with him.

On the street, they hailed a cab. A television inside advertised internationally known deejays playing at places with short, mysterious names—XS, Tao, Pure, Lavo, Tryst.

"I wouldn't mind a little dancing," she said, resting her hand on his knee.

He turned and looked out the window as they moved toward the outskirts of town.

3.   **Petra Jones. Age: 19. Kings County (Brooklyn), NY. 1973.**
     *A cold-water walk-up just south of New Lots Ave. The
     owner of the building has fled to Europe to escape creditors.
     The super has turned the vacant rooms into a cash business,*

charging a few dollars to addicts and panhandlers in exchange for a locked door, the street version of luxury. One Saturday night, a junkie in the midst of a heroin haze flips up the mattress to find Petra. Her body is bloated and burned and faceless. The junkie hurls himself out the window to escape her. He suffers a broken tibia and a shattered collarbone, and the sight of Petra never leaves his mind. Not ever. He sleeps with the lights on the rest of his life.

Twenty years ago, Heath and Shannon had made a suitable match. Heath's parents owned fifteen-hundred acres of productive farmland—mostly winter wheat and corn. Shannon's father, Edgar, was the tractor-supply king of middle Ohio. He'd thrown them the biggest wedding the town of Hamlin had ever seen. Open bar, a Boyz II Men cover band. There'd been only one hitch, and that was when Shannon noticed the rice being scattered all around them as they left the church.

She held up the edges of her satin gown and said, "I wanted bird seed." She turned to Heath. "The birds, they eat the rice and it puffs up their stomachs. They explode. I couldn't bear it if we started off our marriage killing a bunch of birds."

"What do you want us to do?" he said.

"Pick it up," she said. "I want us to pick it up."

So they did, right there in the gravel-strewn parking lot, tweezering the Uncle Ben's rice between their fingertips.

That had been Shannon at the beginning when the world was a spiral staircase ascending into a brilliant and beautiful future. Her resolute and stubborn heart directed them. Heath was rudderless by comparison.

But he knew one thing: he didn't want to go into farming. He even turned down his father-in-law's offer of a sales position selling reapers and tractors.

"It's fine you don't work for me, but you must provide for my daughter," Edgar warned him. "That's a man's job. To provide."

*

Heath became a reporter for the Hamlin newspaper, small-town stuff—basketball games and domestic disputes. Shannon accepted his decision in her silent way, though she made her disappointment clear at his not having chosen a promising vocation. She took a job as a secretary for her father, who paid her three times what anyone else would have made at the same position. Their income was still meager, but none of that seemed to matter when Amelia was born. Their pride and joy, center of their world, bundle of coos and gaws, their little heartbreaker. Years passed—a zipping blur—and Amelia grew. She inherited Shannon's willful nature, became a hellion, an occasional runaway, an unruly and misanthropic teen, a black sheep. It all happened so immeasurably fast.

Then two years ago, when she was nineteen, their beloved daughter went away and never came back. The night before she left, she stood in the living room scowling at Heath. She told him she wouldn't be chained down by his "middle-class, semi-conscious lifestyle."

"You and Shannon (she was using their first names by then) are sheep to the slaughter," she said.

He listened to her spout a lot of other half-baked ideas that young people get after a single philosophy class at the local college.

But she had a point. Who was Heath to say she wasn't right? The year Amelia had turned twelve, he'd plunked down his savings for a stake in the newspaper. Almost immediately, its value began to plummet. Articles and talking heads tolled the "death of print." Now the paper was deeply in debt. He was struggling to keep the house for which they'd overpaid and refinanced twice. Their cars were perpetual lemons. Friends had dwindled over time. He'd taken up a thousand hobbies designed to quash the feeling of discontent he felt in his gut, and he'd abandoned every one of them.

Seeing he wasn't going to respond, Amelia turned and tromped out the door in her heavy biker boots, part of a look she'd been cultivating a whole month.

Heath let her go. God, he just let her go.

He stood there, the door open, the warm breeze trying to fill Amelia's spot in the room.

She didn't return.

Try as he might, he couldn't recall what black-magic words he'd uttered to make her disappear. And not being able to remember meant never being able to take those words back.

The detective they spoke to was a woman with dry hands.

"Your daughter is an adult," she said. She eyed Heath and Shannon suspiciously. "She has every right never to contact you again."

The investigation turned up little.

Shannon stopped going to work, then lost her job.

"I need someone I can rely on," her father said to Heath, "but don't worry, I'll still pay her. I'll still provide for the family. I wouldn't want *my* girl to run away." Then, as if he feared he'd been too subtle, he pointed at Heath and said, "I blame you. Whatever happens to my granddaughter, I blame you."

With all day to herself, Shannon tried to right the situation by beginning a campaign of subterfuge. She caked on makeup to hide her dark-ringed eyes and got rid of the tissue boxes in the house, as if their presence created too much temptation to weep. She constructed a public face, a mask of indomitability. She equipped it with a light smile. She made Heath promise not to say anything to friends, though interaction with anyone outside of work diminished considerably as the months wore on.

Heath, for his part, began combing the internet for word of Amelia. Didn't matter how futile that sounded. He searched. Each night he retired to his tiny office at the back of the house, with its old newspapers and memos and notebooks stacked up around a rickety desk. He fired up the laptop and searched the same news sites that were putting his little paper out of business. The privacy of this endeavor, always with the door locked, double-checked, was to bar Shannon from the gruesome words he punched into the search engines.

nineteen-year-old girl found dead
    —found maimed
    —in coma
unidentified body of young woman
dead girl found with flower tattoo on ankle
girl beaten to death, unidentified
girl stabbed
girl shot
girl raped
girl lost

Sometimes he was wracked with such intense revulsion, such incredible and inescapable sadness at having to write these words, at having to read the accounts which came up as a result, that he pressed a handkerchief hard to his face to stifle the sobs.

4. **Eleanor Lindquist. Age: 14. Dade County, FL. 1995.**
    The De León Hotel. Sixth Floor. For an entire week, the smell is masked by the air fresheners that someone has tucked around her body. Even in the muggy Miami air, which flows into the room when the maids open the balcony doors, it takes another two days before they think to check the bed. One of the maids crosses herself. Entombed beneath the hefty pillowtop mattress is little Eleanor, her small hands laid across her chest, her graying face surrounded by wilted rose petals. She wears a white dress, her shoulders swaddled in a blue blanket. The top of her head is covered with one of the hotel's own towels so that she resembles the Virgin. Another maid thinks to snap a picture. To this day, grainy copies of the Polaroid still circulate up and down Washington Avenue in Miami Beach as sordid little icons for tourists.

For month upon month, he slogged through work in a daze, then trudged home each night to begin his vigil on the internet. Without his noticing, three things happened during this period.

The first was that Shannon came to see him in a different way. By the time a year had passed, she accepted Heath's secrecy. She seemed to prize his newfound singularity. She deferred to him more. On some level, he'd become the man she'd been waiting for, unapologetic about his habits and decisions. They were suddenly able to carry on frank discussions about what they might have done differently. They evaluated themselves, fell into a routine of regular flaying over this or that parenting decision, which kept them contrite and afloat. Yet always they talked as if Amelia were traveling somewhere. Always they speculated what kinds of adventures she was having.

Secondly, during his nightly searches, Heath developed a savvy for the way internet news worked and didn't. He found he had a mind for it. He began making changes in the way the newspaper's online presence operated. He learned terms like "search engine optimization," "cross linking," and "dynamic keyword insertion," things to which he'd never paid attention. None of it was done with some master plan toward better web presence or revenue, but each new change became a boon. In the second year after Amelia's vanishing act, the paper stabilized, grew, and finally turned a profit. It was as if he'd entered into a devil's bargain, his daughter in exchange for the money and career he'd always wanted.

The third event to occur was a secret known only to Heath. A month after Amelia's dramatic exit, he came across the story of a young woman tucked beneath a mattress in a roadside motel in Crowley's Ridge, Arkansas where her boyfriend had kept her hidden away for the purpose of "couple's stuff," as the boyfriend had put it. After she began to rot, the boyfriend left her to be found by the hotel manager.

Heath began seeing other such stories—women hidden in mundane places, spots of stowage and storage—backyard trashbins, bathtubs, floor safes, trunks of cars, maintenance closets, a church baptismal.

Lost-and-found girls, he came to think of them.

But most arresting were those silent and dead beneath the mattresses. Always he imagined them the same. He populated their number with a single face, limp brown hair unwashed, a little acne still extant where her makeup was thickest about the neck and temples. Always the dull green eyes, the trenchant mouth, sharp-edged, supple, and unsmiling. Always the razor-like smirk, the crossed arms that told him, certainly, she would stand there and listen to his lectures, but never would she let any of it, not the slightest bit, sink in.

Every time he discovered one of these particular lost-and-found girls, he wrote a small article from what he could glean. Not an obituary, per se. More an account of the discovery and the circumstances.

The information was usually scant, the women unloved and without enough social cachet to warrant much comment by the media. Usually it was only the oddity of the discovery itself, a woman beneath a mattress, the urban legend playing on every hotel-goer's fears, that made it newsworthy. So he tried to fix the moment of discovery in his mind. He printed his own little write-ups in secret and put them in an envelope on his person so that the unloved girls were always with him.

5. **Jessica Pontain. Age: 26. North Las Vegas, NV. 2001.**
   Scrubbed to a blazing sheen by everlasting light, the Strip bleeds into the night sky, turning it gray from dusk to dawn. On the outskirts of the city, at the edge between darkness and brilliance, halfway between the flickering billboards and the black desert, lies a ceaselessly twilit netherworld, and in it those husks of commerce, the motor lodges, single-storied, rust-flaking signs of dead neon like smiles full of jagged teeth, shot deadbolts in the doors, shabby duvets of outdated paisley. Beneath such a duvet, at the Golden Sunset Motor Court, Jessica Pontain was found, her body racked with the seizures of overdose, twisted into a rigor of eternal fear at some death-minute throes, needle-induced, the vomit dried to a soft white trail down her left

cheek. There is no indication of who cut out the space in the box-spring and laid her within or why. There is no evidence of foul play.

There is only this oddity: it concerns the man who found her.

Allan Pontain, a salesman of medical supplies is driving on Highway 15 from Utah, pulling off at the first place he finds, grabbing a room in the hope of a catching a few hours' sleep. Allan, who hasn't seen his estranged daughter since his divorce fifteen years ago, settles down for the night. He awakes an hour later to find that the dank smell of the room has grown much worse. He drags the night attendant back to his room to search for the smell, and finally lifts the mattress gingerly. The reek ripples upward like a scalding steam and causes the night attendant to run for the door.

In the silent moment that follows, Allan is reunited with the little girl he left behind in Cleveland a decade and a half before. And despite not recognizing her, he knows. Somehow he knows whom he's found.

Two years after Amelia had gone and after every alleyway of possibility had grown dim with shadows, Shannon looked up from an unfunny sitcom and said to Heath, "We should plan a trip."

He'd been dreading this moment. He pictured the two of them going house to house like snake oil salesmen to every residence in the country, Shannon wading through a brief introduction before producing the picture, the one with the marble background from Amelia's senior year. Shannon would flick the photo from her purse like a conjurer producing a queen of hearts. Is this your card? And the person at the door would stare blandly back at them, say no. No, I've never seen that girl. And thus they would move on, interrogating all the people in the country until they died.

"We don't need to go on a trip," he said quietly.

"Yes we do. We need to go to the Empire State Building or the Sears Tower. Do some sightseeing. I want to climb to the top of the Washington Monument and look out those itty-bitty windows."

"Not to search?"

"Search for what?" she said.

He didn't answer. He understood he was in the presence of his wife's unflinching resolve. The same look was on her face as when she made all their wedding guests stoop down in a hot parking lot to gather up rice. But this time her determination wasn't about preserving birds.

"What about Las Vegas," she said. "They have the world's largest Ferris wheel now. You can see for miles. Or the Stratosphere, that giant tower-thingy."

Some part of him understood that she was attempting to climb, to gain height for the sake of a vantage point. She was naming places from which she could scan the landscape for Amelia, an exercise as ineffectual as his own searches on the internet. But he seized the moment. Since finding the account of Jessica Pontain, he'd obsessed over it. Despite the tragedy, Allan Pontain had beaten the odds of distance, time, personality, even enmity to find his daughter again. It was too incredible a coincidence not to believe in a greater network of fate.

"Yes," Heath said. "Las Vegas sounds good."

He and Jezzabelle rode, untouching, in the taxi as the shimmer of the Strip dimmed. The flat, wide streets became desolate the further they drove. The swift wind played across the palm trees positioned like sentinels before the occasional apartment complex. They reached the Golden Sunset Motor Court, and he paid the driver.

As the cab pulled away, Jezzabelle froze in the parking lot and held out her hand. She seemed about to speak, but Heath placed three hundred more dollars in her palm before turning to go in and get the room.

The room was available. On the drive out, he'd been cursing himself for not calling ahead. Room Six. He unlocked it. He let Jezzabelle walk through. Before going in, he glanced up at the Stratosphere, a violent needle of light against the dark. He'd come across other news items. People committing suicide by throwing themselves off the top. How was that possible? To just give up. He'd never understood it, but now he saw death everywhere, its possibilities and history in each structure, room, and highway. Yet what did that make him? Who was he now? Obsessing over the unnatural and violent, scrutinizing the swift and bloody severing of all those perceived trajectories, the history of them bubbling up every few feet. If you knew enough, you knew where death had walked.

He placed the thought aside and entered the stifling room. He flipped on the old AC unit, felt the hot air turn tepid, then stale and cool. She sat down on the bed and slid off her shoes.

"How should we begin?" she said. She patted the spot on the bed next to her. "Take a load off."

He sat instead in the chair by the door.

"I need to show you something," he said. He pulled the envelope from his pocket. The envelope was wrinkled and slightly stained, the unused adhesive a purplish color from lint. He handed it to her.

"What am I supposed to do with this?"

"Read it," he said. "If you don't mind."

She slid out the pieces of paper and read them one by one. He could see her growing uncomfortable, her back stiffening, her chest rising not in a seductive way, but in the way one puffs oneself up so as to appear bigger and more menacing.

"Shit, man," she said.

She didn't run. She looked up at him, placed the lost-and-found girls back in their envelope.

"So what's this mean?" she said. "This a kink thing? You want me to crawl under there?"

He didn't know how to express what he wanted. Other than his wife, he'd never been in a hotel room with a woman. He'd never paid a woman to meet him and offer herself up in whatever way he wanted. In this room, Allan Pontain had found his daughter. Death was being recirculated over and over in the air. A part of Heath knew he could kill Jezzabelle and stuff her there in the same place. It frightened him to know this. Even though she looked strong and was a woman who could defend herself, certainly worldwise, he was a man and stronger, and she was at his mercy. She relied on him not to do things beyond her own choosing.

"I needed someone with me," he said, "to look under the bed. I don't think I can do it myself. My daughter's missing. She turned twenty-one this year, and I'm afraid—"

Jezzabelle rose and opened the door. "Fuck this," she said, but paused in the doorway. "What's her name?" she said. "Your daughter."

"Amelia."

"This is the room, huh? Where the dad found his girl?"

"Lost-and-found girls," he said.

"That's fucked up," she said. "That's really some messed up serial-killer stuff. Is it true? The one about this room?"

"I think so," he said. "I think they're all true."

"That's even more fucked up."

She stepped back into the room. She left the door open a crack so the night air and the sounds of the highway slipped in between them.

"What can I do?" she said. "Couple hundred more, and I'll get over the heeby-jeeby shit."

He realized she was not afraid of him, and reassessed whether or not she had ever been at his mercy. She lowered herself to the floor and placed her hands on his knees. "Lean back," she said. "Is this what you want?" She reached for his zipper.

"I don't know," he said. "I don't know anymore. I just want it to be over." He looked past her toward the bed.

"On the bed?" She rose and sat down on it again, but he was still looking at the mattress.

The room was not how he had imagined. The moment was not how he had envisioned. He was as directionless in this as in all things. His daughter had slipped through his fingers because he wasn't strong, because he couldn't control the outcomes of his life or his family's.

"It's not up to you," she said. Her face changed. Something soft came over it.

He looked up.

"What your daughter did or does. God, that's just like a man to think that way. It's not up to you." She stood and walked to the far side of the bed. "You know what my daddy told me when I was sixteen? He said, Shyla, you ain't ever going to amount to anything but being a whore. And you know what? He was right. My daddy made me a whore by telling me I'd be one. I still blame him for that. But you know what else? He didn't say anything about the other stuff."

"I don't understand," he said.

"I'm a dog groomer," she said angrily.

The statement and its delivery were absurd.

"What?" he said.

"You asshole. I'm finishing school one class per semester. I also run every day. Love it. Five miles or more. I'm a mother. I'm a democrat. I love sardines. How about that? I just found a new house in Green Valley I think I can afford, and I'm moving there so my daughter, who starts kindergarten next year, will be in a better school district. I dream and plan. I'm not dead, and I'm not in need of saving."

He remembered then what he'd said to Amelia to set her off on the night she left. He glanced at Jezzabelle, or Shyla, or whoever this woman was, knowing he'd never know her, even if they became friends, even if they stayed in touch for the rest of their lives.

"I told Amelia something awful," he said. "I told her she was screwing up her life. I told her she was such a screw-up, she'd better hope she found a good man to take care of her."

Jezzabelle stared down at the bed, then tilted the mattress toward him so she was looking beneath it. He could see her shoulders straining to keep the mattress up.

"Do you want me to tell you what's under here?" she said.

"Yes."

"Are you sure?"

"I want to know." He felt tears tickling the edges of his eyes, blurring the features of the room.

"It's a girl," she said. "She's alive. She's happy. She's been living under here a while." Jezzabelle tilted her head as if listening to the girl beneath the mattress. "She has a little story."

Heath leaned forward but didn't rise from his chair. The entire universe seemed to hinge upon his not moving from that spot, not ever actually seeing beneath that mattress.

"She says that when they built the Hoover Dam, there were all these men who fell of the scaffolding into the giant concrete pours. She says there's a legend that the crews were working so fast to complete the dam that those men who fell in were left to die and are still inside the concrete to this day."

She listened again.

"She says that's not true. Everyone of those men was fished out. Some were alive and some were dead, but everyone of them was found and pulled out."

She lowered the mattress.

He shook his head. "I don't know what any of that means."

"Lost-and-found boys," she said. "There are lost-and-found boys, too. It's not just girls. It's everyone. It's all of us. We need someone to find us, and maybe it doesn't matter who. Just find someone and let them know they're not lost anymore."

She looked disgusted with him, as if she'd told every man she'd met this same story and was waiting on just one of them to finally get it. She opened the door and stepped out into the night.

The warm breeze replaced Jezzabelle in the hotel room the way it had with Amelia, but this time Heath didn't stand there. He gathered himself up, took stock in the mirror, and prepared to go. He intended to find his wife and tell her something he hadn't quite formed into words yet. As he shut the door behind him, he could almost hear the whisper of the girl beneath the mattress.

6. **The undiscovered ones. Anywhere County, Anystate. Now.**
They await in the dark for someone to recover them, to treat them with love, to step up and finally protect them, to restore and preserve everything they've lost. They sleep

*silently beneath us all and wait for us to recognize what
we should have known all along—that they are our
daughters, our sons, our sisters, our brothers, our fathers,
our mothers, our friends, our future, and our most beloved,
our yet-to-be-found.*

FRENCH FOR WEAKLING

ON A BACKROAD IN SOUTHERN OHIO, HER VOLVO JUDDERS and pulls like a mule. Whiteknuckling the wheel, she wrangles it off the blacktop into a narrow patch of dirt. All woods and hills, no houses, she hoofs it up to the top of the ridge for cell reception. When the tow truck driver asks if she knows where she is, she tries not to take offense. She always knows where she is. Exactly.

"Eight miles off Green Valley Road on Hooper Ridge Road, headed north toward Highway 32," she says.

The driver snorts. "Shortcut."

"Shortcut," she confirms.

"Take me about an hour to get there. Maybe two. I have to wait on a guy."

She doesn't ask what 'wait on a guy' means.

"Felt like the axle or the bearing coupling broke," she says.

"That right?"

"It's getting dark. I don't see any houses."

"Sit tight. Listen to the radio.

"Might be more money in it if it were sooner."

"Two hours," he says, "maybe longer."

By the light of her phone she returns to the car, its pale features like an old skeleton. The woods speak around her, a crackling and chittering full of mischief. She didn't grow up here, but she's grown familiar. Po-dunk villages in backwater counties—trailers, hollers, piney valleys with dogs chained to stumps near the septic tanks. She always prides herself on knowing her territory, being confident, eschewing the good-natured directions of locals at general stores and gas stations. But the dark—the dark has a way of dissolving familiarity and reintroducing fear. The dark scatters contingency plans and grinds them underfoot. A panic boils up in her stomach, creeps to her neck, and settles in her skull.

She thinks about calling Julius because she can think of no one else. He would oblige her, keep her calm, but he'd see it as one more thing to hold over her head. When this part of the project began, he had offered her a company car, something sporty, and a tidy male intern getting his MBA, a go-getter with a talent for scheduling who might also serve as an unofficial bodyguard. "It's rough country," he said. He paused. "And after last year, I wouldn't want you to be alone and afraid." He said it like he was making a concession for someone whose weakness was barely tolerable. The implication sat between them. But she'd told him no on both counts, to the car and the intern. She would stick with her dependable Volvo station wagon and do the work solo. "You want them to trust me," she said. "No fancy stuff. No extra moving parts."

But thinking now in the dark, amid the lost and wild hills, she hates her daytime self, the one who forgot fear. She wouldn't mind the intern. He would have chattered about an economics professor or a frat party. She would have regaled him with stories from her own MBA, fifteen years ago, a time of her life she remembers better than some events last week or a month ago. Certain moments, she thinks, stand out in relief. They map your life in glittered red high points broken up by dark space.

She draws long breaths, looks out into the oily dark hills. The walls of her heart go all thrippety-jazz, a whole Sunny Murray riff. She cracks her knuckles and opens her purse. In her wallet, she pulls free the blurred picture tucked behind her license.

The photo is black-and-white, printed on cardstock, a little dead girl dolled up to look like the Virgin Mary. It's a crime-scene photo most likely. The girl lies inside a hollowed-out box spring. The mattress that had covered the box spring has been propped up in the corner like a stone rolled away from the tomb. Someone has carefully positioned flowers around the girl, though it's unclear whether this was done before she was hidden or after she was found. There is no accompanying story to clear this up. Six months ago in Miami Beach, a woman on the street selling t-shirts to tourists had whispered, "You want a special souvenir?" The woman offered up the picture. "The Saint of Miami Beach," the woman said.

Terra had handed the woman five dollars, maybe just to make her put the photo away, because the photo was appalling, indecent, something that shouldn't be exposed in public. But, if she were being honest, also because the photograph contained something mystical, something mysterious and macabre. Even if it were a fake, which she suspected it was, it crept up on you, made the hairs stand up on the back of your neck. What had happened here? What kind of person had the little girl been? The picture lacked detail. The mouth, the nose, the closed eyes, the dark eyelashes and the mantle swathed across her forehead were like tiny, impressionistic paint smears. She was as unknowable as the darkness beyond the car. Terra kept it with her because the picture reminded her to be unknowable herself, to maintain a mask while traveling house to house. Let people imprint whatever meaning they need. Let them make a murder into a miracle, a violence into a statement of faith.

Over the past five weeks, she had worked her way into nearly every living room in these parts, and she followed a simple code. Let them make of me what they want. Let them trust. She entered their homes. Women and men, with their worn faces, stared across coffee tables. They were old husbands and wives wearing uniforms after a day's work. A few donned Sunday dress clothes, treating her arrival like they would a dignitary's. Sometimes they invited her to stay to dinner. As best she could, she refused. But some insisted. In such cases, she chewed the ham, shoveled the mashed potatoes, heaped the gravy. She thought of the face of the dead girl. Give nothing away. Anything to get them to trust her.

They treated her like a daughter, like a wife, like a long lost cousin, or long dead acquaintance from dusty school years gone by. She allowed them this, kept her face scrubbed of opinion, of intent. She eased into their lives with deep sighs of warmth. She heard them out, listened, plotted. Anything to get them to sell the land beneath their feet.

Three hours, still no sign of the tow truck. No sign of anyone. She huddles in the front passenger seat. It's early spring and cold. She drifts into unconsciousness, then wakes when a nearby branch snaps. Her heart ramps up again. She stares hard into the dark, catches curt movements in the beyond, the fleeting glimpse of ghostly irises between two trees. She tenses all the way up to her temples before realizing it's a trick of the mind. She's seeing the faint, so faint, reflection of her face in the glass. She's made out the wavering of her own eyes, the tilting of her own head. For just a moment, though, she thought she had seen the little girl, the young Saint of Miami Beach, peeking sweetly from behind a tree.

Confront fear, she thinks. Dash it to ever-loving hell. She opens the door and steps out into the powdery, starch-stiff leaves, which crunch and crumble underfoot. The hill slopes down and away from the car into pooling realms of darkness.

"Little girl," she whispers, and almost laughs at herself.

Stupid, she thinks. She tries whistling The Star-Spangled Banner just to prove she's not afraid. But it feels too loud. She has the acute sense of being locatable to whatever surrounds her. She remembers a man, a kindly gentleman with no wife, whose faltering house smelled vaguely of wet dog, though no dog was evident. She had convinced the man to sign his land away, to give up what was left of his home for the convenience of an apartment in town, but he'd kept her the rest of the afternoon. He'd been one of the insistent, the cloying and clingy, his hand wrapped around the knob of his front door. He'd told her how he used to work on a submarine. "Hotel Seawolf, we used to call it," he said. "'Bout a hundred men in a tuna can roaming the seas."

"Fascinating," she said. She looked at her phone, checking the time to signal she was in a hurry.

"You know most people's misconceptions about submarines?" he said.

"I'm sure I don't."

"They think submarines ping everywhere they go. *Ping-ping-piiiing.* That's all you ever see in movies. The reality? We tried not to ping unless we absolutely had to. That radar sound—we hardly ever used it. This was the cold war. With a ping or two you see what's out there, but you know what else happens?"

She conceded. "What?"

"You let everybody around you know exactly where you are. Maybe, just maybe, you find a Russian sub, but more likely they find you."

She'd nodded and made an excuse to extricate herself from the house. And she hadn't thought twice about what the man said until now. Now she thinks of that *ping*. She thinks of the high-pitched ring of the man's voice. *Ping!* The Star-Spangled Banner dies on her lips. The noise she's made already seems as dangerous to her as a submarine giving away its position in an ocean full of enemies.

She slinks back into the car, silenced, stares into the night. Watches. She sees something. Now nothing. But there it is again. A trembling shadow moving from left to right, sliding through the mist behind the branches. Human, she thinks. The girl. The Saint of Miami Beach in her cheap nativity garb. The girl's body hunching forward. Her form a slight disruption in the upright parallels of the trees.

Then light sends the shadows sprawling. An old pickup rolls in behind her. Its fierce grill nuzzles the back of her car as she steps out and raises a hand to her eyes. In the cab of the truck are two men. Her nerves are riddled. All the worst scenarios roll like freight cars through her imagination: two men on a lonely road with a woman.

"Help you, ma'am?" the driver says as he steps out of the vehicle. He's young, early twenties, his hair blond and wavy, a tad too long. He has lecherous eyes.

"Waiting on a tow," she says.

"Want me to take a look?"

"It's a Volvo."

"So I read." He points at the silver logo near the taillight. "Country boy can't work on Volvos?"

"I didn't mean to suggest," she says.

He smiles. A dimple forms in his left cheek. She'd bet good money that a smile like that works nine times out of ten on whatever young thing he hits up at the pool hall. A shorter man, about the same age with a dark buzzcut, hops down from the passenger side.

"I work on Volvos some," he says. He places his thumbs in his belt loops.

"I'm not going to get rid of you, am I?"

"No, ma'am," the tall one says. "Me and Chad, we weren't raised that way. To leave a woman in trouble."

"I'm not in trouble."

"I'm Erwin," the tall one says. He sticks out a hand. She shakes it firmly. What names, she thinks. What small-town, middle-America names. How could she be afraid of a Chad and an Erwin?

Chad pokes under the hood while Erwin points a Mag-Lite.

"You ever had trouble before?"

"Trouble?"

She thinks about North Carolina, about Raleigh. About Chauncey Rippeth.

"With the car, ma'am."

Chad looks up from the engine. "It's a gasket, pretty sure."

"Isn't that something people say in movies?"

"I don't follow."

"A gasket. A blown gasket or something to that effect."

"It's a problem on the late-nineties Volvos."

"This is a 2006."

"Doesn't mean it's not a problem on this one, too."

"Who'd you call?" Erwin says.

She pulls out the cell. Erwin looks over her shoulder. He smells good—like woodsmoke and a young man's cologne at the end of the day, once it's reached acceptable levels.

"That's Rick," he says, pointing to the number.

Chad makes a noise. "Good luck with that."

"He's not reliable?"

"He'll make you wait."

"He does it intentionally," Erwin says. "Makes people cool their heels so they're in a panic when he gets to you. Then he quotes a price—maybe double what it should be."

"People don't argue," Chad says.

Part of her wants to wait for this Rick, show him who she really is. But tonight, she isn't who she is. She's tired and stranded, letting her imagination slink off to dark places. The little girl is out there, and maybe something else, the wolf that brought her here.

"Is there someone else?" she says. "To call for a tow?"

"You should come with us," Erwin says. "To the house. We won't take no for an answer. It's five miles up the road. Don't let Rick think you're stranded. He'll tow the car. And he won't overcharge."

When she doesn't respond, he says, "It's a plan," and very lightly touches the small of her back, directing her toward the truck.

They turn at a long, gravel drive that delves deeper into the woods. She sits between the boys, swaying and jostling as they make their way over ruts washed out by spring rains. The boys' bodies are equally warm. Chad gives off a different odor than Erwin, more acrid with engine fumes. The house the two boys share is a single-story with gray, wooden siding, even smaller than her condo in Provincetown. Erwin ushers her in like he's making way for a queen. There's a tiny living room with secondhand furniture—a sagging sofa, chipped end tables, a television on an orange, plastic milk crate. To one side is the rattiest La-Z-Boy on the planet.

Erwin retrieves a crocheted afghan from a basket near the television and places it on the back of the couch. "In case you get cold."

"I'm not sleeping over."

"You should," Chad says. Then without conviction, "Might be fun."

"We got weed and some other stuff, too," Erwin says.

She shakes her head.

"Which one of us would you sleep with if you had to choose?" Erwin says.

"I'm not playing that game."

Chad offers beers from the fridge. She declines. The boys each take one and look at her as they drink. A needling angst erupts from somewhere in the center of her stomach. Neck prickling. Skin flush. A bowel-level anxiety. She fights to keep her fingers from trembling. I am in control.

"Have a seat," Erwin says.

She sits on the couch and he plops down beside her. Chad roosts in the La-Z-Boy.

"So where you from?" Erwin says. "Not from here, I know."

"How do you know that?"

"You're too pretty."

"I'm too old for you."

"How old are you?" Chad says.

Erwin slaps Chad's knee. "You're not supposed to ask that."

"It's okay," she says. "I'm not one of those women who goes around pretending she hasn't lived on this earth as long as she has. I'm thirty-seven."

She is thirty-nine but can't sort out exactly why she's lied.

"That's not too old."

Chad smiles. Not as charming as Erwin's. Something gnarled about it. One of his front teeth is slightly more prominent than the other. She tries not to read into it.

"What brings you to our neck of the woods?" Erwin says.

"Property."

"Real estate agent?"

"The details are boring. What about you? What do you do?"

In a horror movie, this would be the point where the two young men reveal that they deal in human organs as they draw their knives.

"I work at Walmart," Erwin says.

"Cabinet factory," Chad says.

"Don't think you can get more boring than that." Erwin stretches his arm over the back of the couch so it rests behind her. "Back to you."

"Let's not talk about work."

Chad's crooked smile makes another appearance. "Okay. What do you do for fun?"

"I hang glide," she says. "Sky dive. Snow board. I'm climbing the world's twelve tallest mountains. I'm on number seven and working my way to number one."

The two boys lean back.

"I'm messing with you," she says.

"Oh," Erwin says. "Well, for what it's worth, I could totally see you doing those things. You seem like an active person."

She is active, she guesses. Cycled the Oregon coast last summer. Planning a three-day hike of the Appalachian Trail before she heads back to DC in the fall. Yet she doesn't want to tell them about these plans. The lies are better. Lies are always power, like unreadable faces.

Erwin grows bolder. "What kind of guys do you date?"

Chad stays slumped back in the La-Z-Boy. This is probably how it goes most weekends. Tall blond Erwin and overshadowed, overly morose Chad at the local bar. Erwin picking up a cutey who's just come in for a drink after nursing classes at the technical college. She imagines them all back here, the light low, Erwin easing his hand into the girl's scrubs, Chad watching them out of his half-closed eyes while he pretends to be passed out on Southern Comfort.

She wants to take Erwin down a peg.

"Guys like Chad here," she says. "That's who I date."

Chad points to his chest. "Me?"

"What do you mean, guys like Chad?"

"You know. Cute guys. Built, but smart. Guys you can tell have a lot going on inside." She points to her temple.

"I'm smart," Erwin says.

She stands. "I need a smoke."

Chad springs. Her fawning has made him agile. He offers her a Marlboro from a smashed soft-pack. Erwin presses down on the cushions like he might stand up and remind her of his height and physique. Maybe he'll smile and reassert his charm. Instead he says, "No smoking in the house, okay? It's just a rule."

She raises her chin at Chad. "You coming?"

Outside, the moon is breaking on a nearby cow pasture. The cow pies are like tiny, squat houses in an ancient civilization. She squints and imagines native peoples in mud huts seen from a distance. There's a little exercise she does where she reminds herself of how all this land was someone else's once. Just about two hundred years

ago, all the unwritten ownership of plains and forests and streams
and fertile hunting grounds changed hands. Whole tribes hustled
off their land with a government decree. And it continues to change
hands, will continue to change hands as long as there are people
looking to make money.

He leaves the porch light off to keep the bugs away. He lights
her cigarette, then his, and they became two orange dots in the dark.
Two blips. She thinks about bright points in the darkness again,
those eclipsing moments of joy, crisis, ruin. Defining junctures
littering a black map seen from satellite.

"Smoking is silly, right?" he says.

"How so?"

"Bad for you, I guess."

"Good for the soul."

"Maybe."

Silence. Even through the smoke, she smells the field, the
manure, the trees. Chad shuffles closer, hesitates, shuffles back. She
sees why Erwin gets the girls. The beautiful get better at seduction.
Their practice compounds like capitalized interest on investments.
The ugly get exponentially less adept.

"I meant what I said, about smart guys. Those are the attractive
guys." She feels like she's doing charity work, instilling right
principles and confidence from which Chad will benefit for the rest
of his life. More importantly, she feels in control.

He smokes down his first cigarette in silence and lights another.

"You don't fool me," he finally says.

"What?"

"Pardon my saying so, but you were scared back there. I saw it,
the way you looked at us when we pulled up."

"Maybe you're not as smart as I thought."

"So I'm wrong?"

"You're no detective."

"My sister's ex, he used to beat her. She had that look."

"I'm sorry about your sister," she says.

"Is that why you lied? About your hobbies?"

"That was a whim."

He hands her the Bic without offering to light it this time.

"It's okay," he says. "If you were scared. I'd be scared, too. Dark road. You being a woman and all."

"You wouldn't know."

"Sure I would."

"It's a question of physical strength. Men's wants. You can't know. You never will."

He hesitates, uncertain and smoking.

"I'm buying up land," she says. "A lot of it. You asked me what I do. I'm buying large quantities of land."

"How much is 'a lot'?"

"A whole lot. It's for a toxic waste site."

She hasn't told anyone, but this young man catching her out in her fear feels like having her skin removed, having nothing left to hide. She needs power again, and for once the truth feels like power. She thinks for a second what it would be like to know this was her last night on earth. No reason, because the world doesn't need a reason to end. What would she do? Would she fuck this kid? That's what people always assume, that, given their druthers, they'd go out having sex. Or would she wander out into the field and stare at the moon till the sun came up? Would she call the few distant relatives she knows, a couple cousins living in Fayetteville, an uncle with heart disease in Tucson? She thinks more likely she'd throw her phone in a lake. She'd wait and witness whatever calamity was to come—fire, flood, or rushing meteors from the blackened sky hollowing out craters and tossing trees as it all went away. That's what would make her happy, she thinks. To see the end of it. The end of power. The death of a little girl is finally nothing in comparison to the death of everything.

"Toxic waste," he says. "You should have gone with real estate development."

"You don't believe me?"

"Not really. Who says 'toxic waste'? Real people don't say 'toxic waste.' Not people who deal in toxic waste."

"Catching me in my lies," she says.

"Your hobbies, those were better. More believable, at least."

"How's this?" she says. "I'm buying up land slowly, from private owners, over a fifteen-month period for a real estate holding company. That holding company will then sell the land en masse that I've acquired to an energy firm with stock in USEC. That's the United States Enrichment Company. This same firm owns a majority share in a hazardous waste removal corporation with steady but so far unremarkable revenue growth. Once the sale of the land goes through, there'll be a bump in stock prices based on speculation. Investor interest will drive up sales, but that won't be the coup d'etat. The same firm will, a week later, confirm a contract with the federal government to dispose of hazardous waste, along with a state permit to do it in this specific area. There'll be a public outcry. Then one of two things will happen. The deal will go through and they'll build a hazardous waste disposal site about eight miles from here, or the state government will realize its mistake in allowing the permit. State and federal representatives will scramble to keep their constituents happy, so they'll marshal the funds to buy out the land and protect their irate citizens. Either way, I and everyone I work for will make a lot of money."

She inhales deeply before lighting the second cigarette.

"You probably don't tell this to everybody."

"Nobody, actually. I don't know what came over me."

"I do," he says.

"Enlighten me."

"You're trying to make me feel small. You know even if I say something, even if I make a big stink, nobody'll listen."

"For someone who works at a Walmart, you're not slow."

"Erwin," he says. "He works at Walmart. I work at the cabinet factory."

"That must explain it."

"You want to feel powerful?" He steps off the porch and holds out his hand. "Come on. Prove you're not a chicken."

"Where we going?"

She doesn't want an answer. She wants him to lead her across the field. She wants not to be scared, for it to be the last night on earth, the way she imagined. She wants to believe they're going together to watch the world burn itself into oblivion. No consequences. She wants to pray to the Saint of Miami Beach as the world bites down with teeth of ash and a tongue of fire.

She takes his hand—it's rough, what else?—and allows herself to be led. He escorts her to the back of the house where a barn stands out against the trees. The barn is very old. Its timbers are heavy, rough-hewn, gray in the moonlight, stippled with knots like the ball joints of old bones. The door swings on a rusty hinge, heavy and unstable.

Inside he flicks on an electric light, though she imagined the hiss of a lantern. There are no stalls like she's seen in other barns. A long unused trough for pigs hangs against the wall. Clumped straw litters a few pens. The place hasn't held animals in a long while.

"What's in here?"

She expects him to show her a blanket where they'll make rough love, where her knees will scrape against the uneven concrete slab beneath the beams. She'll get scabs that snag the legs of her pants for days, little reminders of tonight. She'll allow it, she thinks, the coarse lovemaking in the prickly dirt, the filth in her hair. She'll be outside of herself for a little while. Afterward she'll have her car towed, shack up in a crummy chain motel and think of young Chad fondly, the way he was too quick to come or how he fumbled with the clasp of her bra.

He releases her and disappears through a doorway half-curtained with an old feedsack. A minute goes by. That queasy sense of peril steals up her spine again. She licks her lips the way she did when she was nervous as a child, the way she had in Raleigh when she'd tasted the blood flowing down from her nose and the cuts over her eyes.

"Personally," Chad says as he appears, "I never had much use for it, but I think you might like it."

He's walking backward, pulling a handtruck. On it is a machine like a jukebox. He swings it around and sets it down in the center of the barn. It's one of those old punching machines with what looks like a speed bag dangling from an overhang. A meter of colored lights is displayed along the back of it. A chrome coin slot is positioned in the front.

In chipped paint are slogans in the style of comic-book onomatopoeia:

KNOCK EM OUT!

SHOW 'EM YOU'RE A MAN!

BICEPS!

KNUCKLE MANIAC!

Chad runs the plug to a grimy extension cord. The machine spasms to life. The lights arc up, red blue yellow green, illuminating a cartoon crowd of boxing spectators with cigars and fist-clenched wads of wagered money.

The speed bag raises on its arm, then lowers again.

Chad brings out a mason jar full of quarters and slides one in the slot.

"Go ahead," he says. "Give it a try."

She's unsure. These are not the events she expected. This machine, its sweat stench, is prominent even among the myriad smells of the dead barn. The male-ness of the thing. The appendage hanging down. The ugly knuckle marks and slight tears made by men, undoubtedly and inevitably always men, who for how many decades have pummeled this stupid thing as a way of proving what?

"Go on," Chad says.

"I've never understood the point."

"The point is fun. The point is to kick some ass."

She steps near it. She winds up and punches. The bag is harder than she expected. Its padding is tamped by years of pummeling. She feels her knuckles make contact with the metal bar at its center.

"Shit," she says.

The bag rises. The meter blinks as if calculating her score. The lowest light glares to life. Above it, the words *WIMPY WOMAN!* wink on and off.

"You okay?" Chad says. Half concern, half mockery.

"If you're so strong, you do it."

"Not really fair. I'm an old pro."

"I just want to see your technique."

"Fine," he says, feeds the thing another quarter and waits for it to lower. "Got to keep the wrist straight." He punches, but she can tell he doesn't put his full force into it. His face doesn't change. The meter makes its blinkety calculation and comes up with *NICE TRY, NANCY!*

"Go again?" he says.

She nods, keeps her wrist straight, strikes. This time, a charge rolls up her bicep into her shoulder.

POWDERPUFF! says the meter.

"Again," she says.

LICKING LIKE A LADY!

"Again."

FEEBLE FEMALE FISTS!

"Again."

GIRLY MAN!

Five, six, twenty times, she throws more of herself into it. She grunts, swings wild, carries through. A rage roars up out of her, seethes through her lungs, the sweat boiling off her forehead.

Her anger takes over.

"Again," she says.

DON'T CHIP A NAIL!

Whanging away, killing it, shattering a man's face beneath her knuckles.

SISSY PANTS!

Chauncey Rippeth ripped apart and bloody,

PUSSY!

bones cracking, shattering, slamming,

FEMME FATALE! (THAT'S FRENCH FOR WEAKLING!)

his nose ruined, crammed into his skull in broken bits, his sockets blood-bowls,

STICK TO HOUSEWORK!

one eye dislodged, jaw torn away, teeth tumbling over the tongue, down his throat,

PUSSY!

in a desperate, gagging, violent death.

PUSSY!

"I'm calling it," Chad says.

She steps back, fever-broke, bewildered and heaving.

"Your knuckles," he says. "They're bleeding."

She stares down at her arm. Her wrist feels swollen.

"I was wrong," he says. "You're not scared. You're a stonecold killer."

The room comes back to her slowly in a widening aperture of wood and nails and rusty scythes hanging on a wall. The shadows in the hayloft are dominant and still.

"Stone cold," she repeats.

He smiles at that.

"Fucking thing," she says, and surprises herself by spitting at it.

"Let me show you something," he says.

He finds a two-by-four about five feet long in a corner of the barn. "Stand back."

He loads a quarter and waits for the bag to lower. He holds the two-by-four like a baseball bat. Swings. His triceps tense, the cords in his neck stand out. The board hits hard and the bag shoots up into its nest. The impact rattles the air.

The meter ticks away as the machine thinks it over.

A light at the very top flashes: *NOT BAD! BUT YOU STILL HIT LIKE A GIRL!*

She stares at that. Chad's breathing is the only sound.

"It's a joke," he says. "The whole thing's a joke. No matter how hard you hit, you can't do better than that." He bites down on his lip and shrugs. "You don't prove you're manly or anything."

She wants to explain about her bloody knuckles. She wants to tell him she was serving as a lobbyist for her consulting firm, which in turn represented several corporate interests. Late one Wednesday night a man named Chauncey Rippeth, whose name she didn't know then, stopped her outside the North Carolina Legislative Building where she'd met with a state senator to discuss redistricting. She wants to tell Chad that Chauncey Rippeth smiled at first. But Chauncey Rippeth revealed just enough of a gun in his coat to force her down an alley and do what he wanted. Then Chauncey Rippeth punched her senseless and went home and ordered a pizza. How absurd. How incredibly ridiculous that detail had been and how powerless and futile and stupid she'd felt because Chauncey Rippeth ordered a pizza like it was any other night.

She had memorized Chauncey Rippeth's face without meaning to, memorized the mugshot from a sexual predator database she used to identify him. She fell asleep with that face lingering in the darkness beneath sleep. She only rid herself of Chauncey Rippeth's face when she bought the picture of the dead girl, the Saint of Miami Beach. She wants to tell Chad that by looking into that photograph of that little girl, into its mystery, she suddenly understood that faces were nothing. That faces were whatever people read into them. That her own face means nothing. That a face is a context imprinted by the beholder. A symbol transcribed into babble. You can't help that there is no universal translation.

That was the lesson, she thought. Meaninglessness. Chaos. A fear of the faceless dark.

A spray of light ripples across them through the slats.

"Tow truck," he says.

They traipse back through the yard. The grass is wet with midnight dew.

The tow truck driver drops from the truck, a big man with a beard, somewhat elderly. And she recognizes him from days before. He tips his hat. "Ma'am." This tow truck driver, Rick, is the man who told her about the submarine. Strung up behind his truck is her Volvo. Ping! she thinks. Her car is a submarine whose whereabouts have always been known. She hasn't fooled anyone with her mask, her lies, her face so like the little dead girl.

"You knew it was me," she said.

"I knew, ma'am, yes. And I got to thinking. You seemed in such a hurry the other day, I thought you might need a little time to slow down."

She turns to Chad. "Then how did you know he'd take so long?"

"We didn't," Chad says.

Still trying to process, she says to Rick, "So how much are you going to charge me?"

"I don't know, ma'am. I don't know if it's fixable."

"Fixable," she repeats.

"Could be unfixable."

"That's idiotic. Nothing's unfixable."

Rick looks down at his shoes. Instead of answering, he kicks the dirt. He shoves his hands into his pockets like a chided boy. "That's what I thought, ma'am. Then I sold you my land. You don't suppose that's something that can be taken back?"

"No," she says quietly.

"I didn't think so."

Chad speaks up. "Take it to Burns' Garage."

"You okay with that?" Rick says.

"I can live with it," she says. "If they can fix it."

Rick spits in the dirt, nods once, and climbs back into the cab.

"I'm staying here." To Chad he says, "You'll drive me in the morning?"

"Sure."

"How much?" she asks Rick.

"To Burns'? For you?" He thinks it over, his thumb on his chin. "For you, nothing. You being so good and all about helping me sell my place." He spits in the dirt at her feet.

He looks at her bleeding knuckles before pulling out slowly from the drive.

Inside Erwin has disappeared behind a closed bedroom door.

"I'd give you my bed," Chad says, "but it's a mess. To be honest, probably doesn't smell all that good."

"You're not going to ask me to bed? You don't want me?"

He picks up the crocheted afghan. "Our grandma made this. Sorry about lying."

"Lying?"

"We don't know Rick from Jesus. Erwin saw the listing on your smartphone there when it came up."

"You lied," she says. "To get me here."

"That's what I'm fessing up to. We decided before we got out of the truck we'd tell you something to get you to come with us. Erwin made up the thing about Rick's high prices on the spot. He's quick on his feet like that. We thought maybe we could all party or something."

"Party," she repeats. She doesn't ask what it means.

Chad retreats to his room and, after kicking a few crumpled shirts out of the way, closes the door.

She sits on the couch alone. The adrenaline sluices away from her feet and fingers. Her extremities feel hollow. Her face feels as free of expression as that little girl in Miami.

A month after Terra was assaulted, Julius came to her office. He crossed his legs. "You know," he said. "I think you should come out with it. Advertise the rape. Tell people. Use it. Get some of your power back."

"I've been robbed of my power, is what your saying."

"You're putting words in my mouth."

"No, I think you're trying to put words into mine."

"Let's not make this contentious." He waved his hands in a sign of surrender, but kept talking. "Could be great PR. And, of course, be good for your mental well-being."

"How exactly would publicizing my rape be good PR?"

"You could do some pro bono stuff. Outreach. Front and center for the firm. Build up your face."

"Is it going to take another beating?"

"That's in poor taste. Really poor. Your public face, your persona."

"It's my face," she said. "Why would I want to put it out there?"

"Your next job," he said. "A little unorthodox, but right up your alley. Call it land management." He handed her a thumbdrive. She opened it on her desktop. A seventy-point itinerary of acquisition in southern Ohio. And right at the heart of the plan was her. Ballpark estimate, she guessed the deal might be a hundred million, maybe more. She'd be the agent on the ground, the phalanx spearheading their attack.

"You have big plans for me," she said.

"Big," he said. "And if this goes south—if we do take a PR hit?—you'll be the one to explain to the public. The lady who fought back against sexual violence, she'll assure people it's okay—"

"To rape the land instead."

"You're sharp," he said. He tapped her desk and stood, looking down at her. "Maybe getting fucked did you some good." The charm had gone out of his face. "You'll do this, the rape-prevention thing. Go to a battered women's shelter. Do a few speaking engagements. Perform. I've already set it up through my secretary. There'll be photo ops and press. We'll write it up. Then you'll go to Ohio and start buying. It's not really a request."

She pulls the afghan over her shoulders and pretends to sleep. A couple hours pass. Dawn fills up the windows. She looks at the picture of the little dead girl again, the Saint of Miami Beach. The trip to Florida was for a speaking engagement at Miami University as part of a Title IX conference, all part of Julius's grand plan. She moderated a panel discussion of high-profile businesswomen who were speaking out about harassment and sexual assault in the workplace. She was exhausted by it. Young women, college-aged, holding up their hands, delicately plying her with questions meant to sound abstract but which were all too evidently personal, so personal. She hated these young women for being weak, for not just spitting it out. I've been . . . say the word. Say it.

She didn't want to be an icon. She didn't want to be unfixable in the eyes of everyone who now knew. After the panel, she'd roamed Miami Beach in a haze. The picture of the little dead girl that had been offered to her had emerged out of nowhere, like all the faces of those young women in the crowd. But the dead girl's face was pleasantly blank, a reminder, certainly, but also a respite. The little dead girl didn't want answers. She was one.

She walks onto the shoddy porch where she and Chad smoked in the dark. The afghan feels heavy around her shoulders. Of all the moments, the big and recent moments, this will be the one that stands out in her mind in the months to come. Because right here she makes the decision. And with that decision, it feels like everything comes rushing up silently through the fog, through the dew-dark roots of the trees, through the silent and sallow broomsedge wagging in the morning wind. This is the moment she will remember.

Within six weeks, the deal on which she's spent so much time will fall through. The legislature will indefinitely ban the right to dump hazardous materials in this part of the state by pushing a hasty park designation across a swath of pivotal acreage.

This is the moment. Now. Half-consciously clutching the afghan, looking over the pasture. She steps off the porch and returns to the barn. She finds the punching machine. It's already dusty somehow in its corner surrounded by mouse droppings and scattered hay. She forms a fist, cracking the scabs over her knuckles. She squeezes herself behind the machine and opens a rusty panel on the back. Inside is a surprisingly stark filigree of colored wires. Small bulbs are mounted on a wooden form. She removes each bulb carefully and scatters them on the ground. Then she stomps them to crystalline bits that sparkle in the dirt and dried manure.

A week will go by before she leaks the first word of her mission to one newspaper and one television station, both with enough influence to raise a stink. Another week before she intentionally blows the deal with a farmer who owns a hundred acres dead center of the company's intended development land. After that, most of the dominos will fall without her help. The legislature, in a rare show of bipartisan prowess, will act swiftly. Her holding company, and by proxy her firm, will be left holding a patchwork of disconnected plots, which they will have to siphon off for a fraction of the purchase price. One of these plots a man named Rick will buy back for half of what he sold it. All in all, her investors will lose close to fifty million.

She'll be fired, of course. But with a hefty severance package. The company will find it in its best interest not to summarily shortchange the woman who made a name for herself by talking about, among other things, disparity in the workplace.

In those months to come, she remembers that morning, the morning after her car broke down. Treading back through the high grass toward the porch to find Chad standing there with a hot cup of coffee in his hand, that half-snaggled smile on his face as he held out the mug. He produced a small cardboard box from under his arm.

"You'll want these," he said. "To finish her off."

He pried up the top on the box and poured its contents out at her feet. Forty or fifty more glass ovoids with their silvery, threaded bottoms rolled out like pill bugs trying to escape. "Replacement bulbs," he said, and brought his boot down slowly. The bulb beneath it made a satisfying pop followed by a crunch that seemed infinite. He slammed his other boot down on a second one.

Startled, she laughed. Then brought her knee high up to her chest and obliterated one, two, three.

He laughed loudly.

Then they both clomped and stamped and jumped and giggled, decimating the whole mess of bulbs until tear-drop-sized bits winked in the sun and Erwin came out in nothing but a pair of shorts.

"Sheezus, what the hell you guys doing?" He looked down at the shards and twisted bits of metal strewn across the porch. "Sheezus," he said again, which made her laugh harder, and Chad along with her.

She thinks of this moment, guffawing and leaping up like children, feeling alive in the new warmth of morning, feeling unafraid and assured. She thinks of it her entire life. Especially when the weather takes a turn and the bright sky goes a yellowy green all charged with lightning. She stares out over the land she kept for herself, one of the farms she acquired not six miles from that porch, and those details—the devastation of glass at her feet, the sound of her own childlike happiness, the way her cheeks ached to hold such a wide and goofy smile for so long—those details now feel like parts of a larger strand, blips flickering to life in a string of brilliant moments.

EGGS AND BACON
AND COFFEE

IT ENDS WITH CLEATS AND TEETH. GRASS CHURNED IN SOLID green chunks. The thrill of turf flying behind as he rushes down the field. The awful silence of the crowd in the stands. The barking huff of defenders giving chase. And wind. Most of all, wind. A white constant flowing and flowering through the earholes of his helmet as below it, like a bassline, the shoulder pads chug away with every step. His heart lifting, the blood pumping, the sudden thrill of being alive.

Started ten weeks ago with a towel on the bathroom floor. A fifteen-year-old boy, long-limbed, frowsy from sleep, wearing nothing but boxers. Stopping mid-yawn to stare at what looked like a dead dog near the toilet.

Rain cascaded down the wall through a leak in the side of the trailer. The water had collected in a rust-smelling puddle and rotted the plywood beneath. Three weeks previous, Darla's boyfriend, Jake, had drilled a half-inch hole through the floor. That was Jakes' solution to the stagnant, cold pool between tub and toilet—a makeshift drain that allowed beetles and ants and wasps and cockroaches to climb up into the bathroom at night.

Darren toed the soggy terry cloth, kicked it aside and stomped. The boards bowed, spongy underfoot. Darla, he figured, must have thrown the towel down in the night. He checked the closet and found exactly what he expected to find. Nothing. No washcloths, no towels.

He showered and drip-dried, which made him late, the bus honking, the other kids snickering as he tromped to his seat. At school, he sat in shop class. Biology, algebra, English, American history. He zoned out some. Cortez was cool. Conquistadors had badass armor. He added a Bane mask to update the style. Sometimes he thought he'd be an accountant. He thought about the mudrunner he'd buy with his money.

This is common. Darren's court-appointed visits to me were nothing if not reiterations of the same old fantasies and frustrations. Maybe it's why I'm trying to put them down here, in hopes you forgive him the ending. I want you to understand the moment on the football field.

Leaving school, Darren noticed Jake, parked behind the buses. Jake was twenty-six and could have passed for one of those losers that stick around to finish a final PE credit. He rolled down the window of his pickup.

"Your mom's in a fit. She don't find it funny you plugged the hole."

"What the fuck you talking about?"

"Watch your mouth. School property." Jake pointed at the buses. "You covered the drain hole with your towel. Rained all morning and flooded the bathroom into the hallway."

Darren felt his spine weaken. As punishment for the truancy officer's letter about "excessive" absences, Jake had come by and whipped Darren with a six-foot coaxial cable. This'd be worse.

"I'm staying. Got football," Darren said.

"Since when you play football?"

Mr. Jenkins, the transportation coordinator, approached Jake's truck. "This is the bus area. You have to go around to the parent pick-up area." He turned to Darren. "You two related?"

"I got football," Darren said.

He was spared a few hours, is how I think of it. I asked him why he'd gone. Why he hadn't dodged football for something else? Smoking behind the school? Walking around in one of the neighborhoods nearby?

Darren told me he thought that Jake might follow up with one of the coaches. He also reasoned Darla might be on board with an extracurricular activity. The few times I met her, she talked a good game. She knew the language of good parenting.

As to why he stuck with it, I think it was a reason to stay out of the house.

Back in the spring, to get out of Earth Science, Darren had gone to the meeting for guys interested in football. He'd kept the forms in the bottom of his backpack. He'd signed them at his kitchen table by tracing a returned check Darla got from the grocery store. He handed the papers to the head coach, Rinehart, who told him not to expect much.

"You missed all summer," Rinehart said. "I shouldn't let you play at all."

Darren looked at his feet. "Ain't got cleats."

Rinehart spit into a nearby trash can. "We'll find you an old pair."

That was that.

Half hour later, he was on the bright green field marred brown in patches by the practice teams. The assistant coach looked him over and said he was outside linebacker material.

"You quick?"

"Quicker'n most," Darren said.

The coach dumped him with eight other guys doing drills. They ran sideways and backward and sprinted forward. After that, they practiced picking up a football that another coach, Layton, threw on the ground. The boys scooped the ball into their arms and ran with it, then jogged back while Layton yelled and slapped their pads. The first few times, Darren muffed the ball, tripped over it. The other guys laughed. Coach Layton roared and said Darren shouldn't have missed two-a-days.

The fifth time, Darren scooped the ball and ran. He felt the ball tucked tight and safe against his side. When he hustled back and tossed the ball, Coach Layton clubbed his shoulder and said, "Finally!"

Darren did it again. He did it again, then again. He could do it all day. *This is what he told me.* He got faster each time. The ball seemed to want his fingers, to jump upward into his arms and nestle against his ribs. Then the coaches blew their whistles and it was on to tackling drills.

Hitting the ground as he wrapped his arms around another boy or another boy around him, or trying to outrun the other boy or have the other boy juke and shuffle sideways to get past him, these were all good things. They didn't hurt the way Darren always thought they might. His arms skidded in the grass, and a great wallop of the helmets sounded all around his skull when he collided with the others. He did it harder and harder to test the pain. None of it was like being whipped. None of it like hot cigarettes or broken glass. And after a while, when the other boys saw how hard he hit, they smiled. They breathed in great huffs, sprang up from the ground and shook off the pain into the dry, yellow grass where they'd gone down. They did it all over again, as many times as the coaches demanded.

"Shit," said a boy with an eighty-eight on his chest. "You hit like a fucking wrecking ball for a skinny guy."

At the end of practice, they ran. The running was endless. They ran in great groups all lined up. They sprinted to one end of the field. They turned around and raced. Again and again. The pads felt like bricks, but Darren kept running. When he looked around, only a few of the boys were with him. He wasn't the fastest, but he was close.

I tell you the rest in strictest confidence. After practice, Jake used a rake handle, newly broken. He came when Darren was asleep and used a rake handle.

Darren had a sister. Betsy charged thirty dollars to suck cock. She had a dark blue Escort she parked in the gravel lot behind Smitty's on Thursday nights when she wasn't working at CVS. She read *World of Warcraft* novels and pulled occasionally at her coat. The coat had a broken zipper. Every so often a middle-aged drunk stumbled out and knocked on her window. The drunks always scanned the edge of the parking lot, then slid into her passenger seat. A moment later her head would dip below the dashboard. Ten extra dollars to take her top off and let them fondle her. She tried to make it last at least ten minutes.

Darren made certain she was alone. He crouched behind his sister's car and pounded on her trunk.

"What the hell?" She scrambled out, her hands cinching her jacket against the wind. Her eyes were bloodshot, her nose red from the cold. She was five-two, maybe ninety pounds or a hundred.

I met her once. Small with sad eyes.

Darren stood up and smiled. "Gotcha. You think it was an axe murderer?"

"It's cold," she said. She gestured to his t-shirt and gym shorts. He liked not wearing enough. It made him feel strong against the temperature. His chest was already broader from weightlifting. Less than a month in football, and he'd packed on considerable muscle. He pounded his chest.

"Not cold at all," he said.

"Well, I am. Get in."

"I'm not sitting on the jizz throne." He pointed to the passenger side.

She ducked back in and slid over. He shut the door and examined the car like he might find evidence of the men who'd been here, a pair of pants strung across the dash or an old-timey fedora perched on the back of the seat. He ran his fingers down the steering wheel. "How much you think I'd need to save for a car?"

"That what you came to ask?"

"You gotta punch a clock?"

"You shouldn't be here. What happened to your cheek?"

A long bruise ran from the corner of his mouth to just above his ear. We were meeting regularly then, and I saw it. He told his teachers it was football. He'd told the coaches he'd slipped on the stairs. It wasn't inventive. They all said they believed it. With Betsy he didn't make up an explanation. Her question was rhetorical. He learned that phrase in school—a rhetorical question. Rhetorical, historical, oracle, chortle. To Darren, rhetorical meant the response didn't matter—you could say anything, gibberish or whatever— because the answer was already set. Beyond your control.

"How do you know if a chick likes you?"

Betsy laughed. He liked making her laugh, even at his expense.

"What'd she say?"

"Who?"

"God, you're dense."

"She said she liked my jersey."

The entire team wore their jerseys on game day. Jennifer Holloway had tapped her teeth with her pink-painted fingernail before telling Darren he looked good. As a result, he wore the jersey the next Monday and Tuesday until one of the other players scolded him. That was only a Friday thing. Don't you have any other clothes? the guy asked.

But Jennifer Holloway.

Darren tumbled the syllables of her name across his tongue until they were greetings or grunts or tuneless songs. Jennyver Hollowweigh. Hello, way. Hell, Jennifer Holloway.

Jennifer Holloway was probably rhetorical, too.

"She likes you," Betsy said.

"Serious?"

"If she said anything, she likes you."

He wanted to take his sister out for supper, to a nice diner. He'd pay for eggs and bacon and coffee and talk it all over. He had some money. Fifteen dollars for raking leaves for the neighbor, who was elderly and had a milky eye. *Her name's on the tip of my tongue.*

"Want to go somewhere?" he said.

"Don't start," Betsy said. She thought he was teasing her. Three men that night had already asked her the same question. "Not funny. Get out."

Jennifer Holloway, he thought. My sister Betsy, he thought. He would take them out and buy them food. They'd laugh at his jokes.

Or maybe that was rhetorical. Maybe the words didn't matter and he'd never get them all in a diner.

Diner, piner, shiner, he thought.

Autumn died early that year. First week of October, a shy snow fell, tickling the grass on the field and making the fresh white lines hard to see. Boys stuck their hands in their pants to keep them warm. They made dick jokes. Don't play with it between plays! You'll break it off!

Five weeks playing and Darren was always on the sidelines during games. The thrill of practice and his speed and the grin beneath his translucent mouthguard were nothing—because the games were what it was about, and he didn't get to play in the games. He was a sophomore, they said. He'd get his chance. But in his heart he knew he was better than the others. He saw the coaches believing it but resisting their own minds. During games he watched their heads in their headsets waggling left and right, him waiting for them to turn and say, Go in. Go. Go in and run. Go in and take the ball away from the other team and run. Run and run until the crowd cheers your name.

It was always about running. He'd give me a look and he'd slap the back of his calves to show me how strong they were. Sitting across the desk from me he'd smile and tell me he was fast. I'm fast, he'd say. Real fast.

Jennifer Holloway said she thought Darren was cute. He stood on the cement steps outside the high school and asked her out. She said, Sorry. Sorry. I think you're cute though. I have a boyfriend already, she said. A boy at another school. And the rest was rhetorical because his stomach sank into his balls.

But cute. I'll fuckin take cute, he thought. I'll take cute. Other girls roam the halls.

That night he came home to find Darla sitting on the coffee table with a plastic bottle of gin between her knees.

"I'm not drinking," she said. "If that's what you think."

"I didn't say nothing."

He walked toward his room.

"Better get out," she said. "I'm going to burn this place to the ground. I'm dumping this on the couch here and setting it on fire."

Betsy had started working part-time at an insurance office. The plump woman who owned the place asked Betsy for the names of all her relatives and signed Darla up first thing for insurance on the trailer. Twelve dollars a month.

"Don't be a cunt," Darren said. "The insurance company would know."

Darla threw the bottle at him. He dodged it, easy, kicked it toward the kitchen and watched it skitter across the torn linoleum.

"Got to try harder than that," he said.

Later, while he slept, Jake snuck into his room with a thick phone book. "Disrespect your mama," Jake said, "and you're disrespecting me." He held the phone book over his head and thumped Darren with it. "I learned this from a cop show," he said. "It don't leave marks." He hit Darren again and again with all the names of all the people in the town.

More weeks went by. The snow came. The snow gave up. A little reprieve. The grass lifted in the shallow warmth of middays in November. The brittle grass. The yellow grass. The field crew made signs: Keep OFF. Keep OFF the GRASS, to let students know an easy way to rebel.

Jennifer Holloway kissed her boyfriend. During practice, Darren stared across the field and saw the boy picking her up from school. They fit together, he and her, like two sides to an archway, leaning from the driver seat, from the passenger seat, touching lips. Darren thought of his sister and the diner he never took her to.

Two days later he performed a tacking drill with another boy and broke the boy's arm. This made Darren feel good. *He told me so.* The boy was the starting outside linebacker. The other boys stood quiet while the paramedics drove their ambulance across the field. The ambulance left long brown ruts where the linebackers practiced. Then the boys ran. Their running was a silent thing in the dimming light.

More weeks, and another boy took the first linebacker's spot. Darren was faster than the second-string boy, but the second-string boy had a father who owned three convenient stores in town. Darren thought, shit. He thought, that's about right. Faster is rhetorical when someone's dad owns three convenient stores.

About this time, Darren's court-mandated appointments finished up. I didn't speak to him until a month after the final game of the season. By then, the game had become a sordid bit of gossip in the town's history.

The night before the game, Darla hacked up blood and Darren walked her two miles to the ER at the clinic because Jake was out with the truck. Plus an ambulance costs a shit-ton of money. The doctor asked if Darla had been sick, and Darla said, "My whole goddamn life."

The doctor, who was bald and had a pointy skull, looked at the pack of cigarettes sticking up from Darla's purse. "Yep," he said. He told Darla a nurse would come.

Two hours later, and no nurse, Darla had one of her fits of martyrdom. "You go, baby," she said to Darren. "Go get rest before school. You got a game tomorrow."

"Fuck that," he said.

"Watch your mouth," she said. "You're in a hospital." She placed her hand on his cheek. Her palm was cool and there were wrinkles on the inside of her fingers. Darren could feel them against his skin. "You go home for momma. Kay, baby? I'll be fine. I'll give you a call if it turns out to be anything. You tell Jake I'm okay."

"Fuck Jake," Darren said.

"Don't be that way," she said. "I didn't raise you that way."

She touched his shoulder with her fingers. He could feel her getting older. Seconds were years, were decades.

"Go home," she said. "Get on." She shooed him.

On the way back he passed the place where they tore down the old foundry. He slipped under the fence with the sign, KEEP OUT, KEEP OUT DANGER, and found a piece of rusty rebar with a hunk of block still cemented to the end. It was like a Viking weapon or a conquistador thing. Braining Indians. Tearing down pyramids that stood for thousands of years.

He arrived back at the trailer and waited an hour with the rebar in his hand.

Despite the second job at the insurance agency, Betsy still sat outside Smitty's. Stunted trees bordered the back row of cars in the parking lot, and Darren pushed through, still carrying the rebar. He stood before Betsy's car and watched her go down on a man. The man tilted his head back on the headrest and stared at the ceiling. The dim blue light sliced in through the windshield and made it look like the top of the man's head was missing.

Darren tapped on the passenger-side window, but Betsy didn't stop. Darren kicked the door, and she rose up, then climbed out. She was shivering as she pulled on her jacket.

"What the fuck, Darren?"

The man in the car stepped out and buckled his pants. He wasn't ashamed. He was tall. His bloated gut was an entity.

"Little fucker," the man said.

Darren swung the rebar at him. The swing wobbled. The weight was awkward. The man blocked it. He punched Darren in the jaw, and Darren fell. He dropped the rebar. The man kicked him in the shin with the heel of his workboot.

"Little fucker. Little fucker."

"Stop it," Betsy screamed.

Another man called over.

"Nothing," said the tall man. "Little fucker tried to rob me."

"That's bullshit," Darren said.

The man kicked him in the ribs. "I should kill you." He snatched up the rebar and hurled it into the brush.

"Shit," said the man. He threw a twenty at Betsy. "Don't say I didn't pay."

*

A part of me thinks Darren is lying about the man's payment. To make himself feel better about losing her the money.

The paper placemats at the diner were the whitest things on earth. Someone had shipped that whiteness from China on the other side of the world and left it here beneath a bowl of soup on a gray formica tabletop.

"Why you such an asshole?" Betsy said.

The soup wasn't what he wanted. There should have been a plate of eggs and bacon. There should have been Betsy and Jennifer laughing. But Betsy had ordered soup because his mouth was swollen.

"You cost me," she said.

The fight had gone out of his chest.

"I's going to kill Jake," he said.

Betsy kept staring.

"Never showed," he said.

"You don't need to fight him. Whyn't you just leave it alone?"

He sipped the chicken noodle soup, which had cooled.

He mumbled something.

"Good luck with that," she said, and crossed her arms.

Last game of the season. Not a shred riding on the game. The team had missed their chance at regionals three weeks before. Last game of the season, and they were whipping the opposing team's asses by three touchdowns at fourth quarter.

Coach Rinehart waved his arms like he was parting the Red Sea. "Send in second team," he said.

So Darren was in. He was fast and he was in and there was nothing important about the game.

"Fuck," Darren said as he jogged onto the field. He watched the boys on the other team in their bright purple jerseys. The play started. Darren dove. He collided. He tackled. The boys on the other team were slow. He hated them, they were so slow. He eyed the boy with the ball, a short, thick running back with a black visor in his facemask that made it so Darren couldn't see his eyes. The other team gave the ball to this boy, the fullback, and Darren tackled him, but the boy wouldn't give up the ball. The boy was slow and strong. He held the ball in a death grip and pushed for a few yards.

Another down. And another. Between plays, the boy with the visor heaved white breaths through his mask. Darren wanted his own superior speed to mean something, to catch the boy in the backfield and make the other team move backward. But the other boy wouldn't stop. Even when Darren reached him first thing, right at the line, the boy charged a few yards more. The boy became Darren's enemy.

Enemy, he told me.

The other team moved forward. A first down. Another. Darren's team was being backed up. They were being pushed until it was the sixty, the forty-five, it was thirty, then only fifteen yards left, and the other team could see the endzone. The boy with the visor breathed. Darren breathed. They were brothers—*he said that also*—the two of them, hitting again and again on the field.

Like brothers.

A timeout was called. The coach of the opposing team strode out from his sideline. He held up his hand to let Coach Rinehart know he was coming over. Coach Rinehart removed his headset and jogged to the middle of the field to speak with the other coach. They nodded as they talked. They called for the referees. The two coaches and the referees spoke to one another. The referees nodded. Yes. Yes. Yes.

When the talking was done, Coach Rinehart made his way to the huddle where Darren and the others waited.

"All right, guys. You played great. Now I want you to do something even greater." Rinehart rubbed his hands together. "Boys, I want you to let them score. We got less than two minutes left in this whole season and you boys get the opportunity to do the best thing we've done all year." He pointed toward the other team's bench. "They got a boy over there. Usually he's a towel boy. He's autistic.

That means he can't play regular football. He's got things wrong with him. But that boy loves this game as much as me and you. And we can give him the chance of a lifetime. We can let him play. You got me?"

The boys nodded. Yes. Yes. Yes.

"They'll hand that boy the ball. They're going to run the play half speed. I want you to let that boy score a touchdown. You hear me?"

Yes.

"Be proud, boys," he said. "You should be proud."

He hoofed it back to the sidelines, and the referees blew their whistles. The crowd cheered. The other team lined up. The boy with the black visor stood on the sidelines. He clapped for the autistic boy who'd taken his place.

Even in his uniform, the autistic boy looked different. He didn't crouch down like the others. He stood straight up like a boy watching butterflies.

The quarterback took position behind the center.

Darren watched the boy who had autism. The boy's fingers tapped his thigh pads. One two three. One two three. One two three.

The quarterback gave his cadence. The center hiked the ball. The boys all stood up. The two teams touched each other. Their hands rose in automatic gestures, little touches, versions of the hitting they'd done all night.

The quarterback dropped back. He stuck the ball in the autistic boy's breadbasket, just like in a real play. It was automatic, this motion, to place the ball where it was most protected. But the autistic boy didn't know how to take care of the ball. He didn't know how to hide it away with his arms and the tight grip of his fingers. The quarterback helped him, positioned the boy's forearms around the ball so he shielded it like an infant.

The quarterback slapped the autistic boy on the shoulder pads. Go. Go. You're doing great. Go.

The line made a hole.

The boys in the backfield, the linebackers, the free safety. They all clapped.

The autistic boy smiled beneath his mouthguard. His cheeks bunched up inside his helmet. He began to run. The crowd rose to its feet, shouted, stomped. Louder than any touchdown, louder than any touchdown all season.

The autistic boy loped—halting, awkward steps, like a boy who'd never run before. He was slow. He was running.

The fifteen. The ten. The five.

Before Darren hit him.

Darren struck the boy with his full weight. He planted his helmet against the boy's chest the way he'd been coached to do. The impact was not like with other boys. It was a feathery thing. A helpless, unready body collapsing under Darren's. The two of them landed together in the grass and the ball skittered out from the boy's grip.

Darren rolled over and rose to his feet, already at a dead run as he scooped the ball and tucked it away and made it safe. He was down the sidelines, knees pumping, feet clawing, propelling. He was light as air. Fast in the tomblike silence of the crowd. He heard the footsteps behind him. The breathing. A curse. The wind. Then nothing. Because they couldn't catch him. That feeling of being pressed against his own goal line fell away. The ache was already in his lungs. He was too fast. The field opened up. It was glorious. All of it. So incredible, such a feeling, every second, glorious.

TRUTH BE TOLD

Truth be told, before he met Jeanine, there were some nights Edward played early Rod Stewart songs and crooned them aloud to his bristlenose catfish, a bottom feeder content to live its life skimming the floor of its tank.

"You're in my heart," he sang quietly—sometimes so low the words barely left his lips. "You'll be my breath should I grow old."

He did it because there was no one else to sing to. He was a soft man, soft-spoken, a droner, a party fixture without bells or whistles. Around Christmas at Proctor & Gamble mixers, you'd find him slumped by the punch bowl with the blanched-looking interns and featureless copywriters.

He's forty this year, and he's catching Jeanine just in time. Forty-one, to Edward, seems outdated, wifeless and alone. But forty—there's still hope. He met her at a line-dancing night for singles at the honky-tonk bar off 32, the Steel Pony. That night he mustered some seriously mystical wooing voodoo. He charmed her, made her laugh, walked her to her car, and pecked her on the cheek. He was everything he'd not been his entire life.

Four dates in, he's enthralled. It's like walking on cotton candy. The AC is out in the diner, the doors open, but the jukebox works like gangbusters, a rickety and raucous reverberation in the speakers. Little Richard bangs out "Long Tall Sally" as Jeanine hums along, releasing the *wooo-ooooo-oooo*s in tender whispers. Her hair is pulled up furiously into a rumpled bunch. She fans herself with a menu and sighs. She's thirty, pale-lipped, with slightly rounded cheeks.

"You should come with me," Edward says. "To North Carolina. I apologize for the short notice. But I've had it planned for months."

Truth be told, he's had it planned longer than that. For the past eight years he's taken the same vacation. Same beach house. Same week of August. All alone.

"I'm a bartender," she says. "I take off when I want. If they fire me, big whoop, there's plenty other places that want my combination of talents."

"What's your 'combination of talents'?" he says.

"I can mix a perfect rye Manhattan, and I have these." She cups her breasts and gives them a bounce.

Edward's stomach goes jello-ey, his head swims. He's imagining her naked, and he figures if they go away, the implicit understanding will be clear. But he's nervous. He doesn't have what you'd call a heap of experience. He's thinking about this, but now he's also thinking about her job.

"I thought you worked with animals," he says. "You said you worked with animals."

"I've done a little bit of everything," she says. She waves her hand in the air like she's cutting through cigarette smoke.

He wants to press further. They've kept it light, and he still knows relatively little. But the other part of him, the carnal and desperate part, the giddy, little id that's been tucked away in the beating, pink parts of his soul, is steering the car now. It's veering headlong around the curve of understanding—yes, she said; Y-E-S.

They'll leave in two days and, he thinks, they'll defile every room of the house.

Truth be told, she used to dream of being a veterinarian. She worked in a vet's office briefly, but she lacked the schooling, and most of her days were spent cleaning cages. She sometimes held dogs as they drifted off under the anasthesia, never to wake up again, while their owners cried or walked out without saying a word.

She does something strange on the way down. It's nine hours to Oak Island from his house in Ohio. They start early, and it's just past noon when they reach the midpoint. He taps the dash and says, "No turning back now. We're halfway there!"

She's asleep and doesn't respond. He nudges her. She turns and snarls. She bares her teeth, snaps them like a hyena. For a second he thinks she'll tear into his shoulder. Then she slams back against the door, inhaling sharply. Her head strikes the window.

"Are you okay?" he says.

Her eyes, wild and searching, close. They reopen with an exhausted sort of calm. Her shoulders, which were up around her ears, melt downward, leaving her neck looking long and sensuous. In the v-neck of her t-shirt, her cleavage is visible. Her chest is tan in a way that suggests to Edward topless sunbathing. He's overcome by this vision of her undressing on the roof of her building. His mouth goes instantly dry.

"Were you dreaming?"

She slides down into the seat. "Sure," she says. "I was a lion."

"You hungry?" he says.

"Nah. You're a big boy, and I'm a grown-up gal. We can make the trip without stopping for food. Don't you think?"

Truth be told, he has a ritual. He stops at the Cracker Barrel just outside Winston-Salem for lunch. He does this on the way down and the way back. Eight years he's maintained this routine. In fact, now he thinks about it, the drive and the dinner might be his favorite part, slicing down through the United States in a luxurious show of personal freedom. He watches a fair amount of the History Channel and, as a result, thinks about the hard fought liberties allowed him through the suffering and moral fortitude of American men and women, all so he can depress the accelerator, feel the fuel pumping through the engine, a stirring vibration underscoring the catchy rhythms of new songs on the radio.

But oh. His breath judders in his throat. Her hand is on her thigh, which is brown like her breasts. A new wave of longing overcomes him. This year's different. Routine is out the goddamn window. Stopping to eat is *most definitely* wasting time. This year, the getting there is one-hundred-percent the point.

A delicate, white star emerges from the grass.

Truth be told, if the beast had any knowledge of such things, it would call the star *painted trillium*. It would call the flower's arms *petals*, its tuft of splayed knobs *stamens*. Had the beast self-awareness, she might call herself *deer*, might classify herself as a *whitetail*. She might note her own thin but powerful legs, and her tawny fur, which has gathered burs in the undergrowth. She might bend the trillium down with her forehoof to admire the slender stem bowing gracefully, the crimson-stained center (which, to her, appears only as a hazy gray), before eating it whole.

But had the deer such a consciousness, she would also register the sound of *squirrel* as precisely what it is, rather than perceiving the flicked twig under the squirrel's foot as a sign of danger. Had she these powers of observation, she would not bolt, not flee all fleet-footed up the timbered trail. She wouldn't charge headlong through brambled forest toward the black swath of asphalt smelling of burnt diesel, acrid oils, and exhaust.

The deer—had she known the flower, had she known the squirrel, had she known herself—might have named the boundary road, might have stolen road's power with her naming, like Adam from the Bible, might have fixed dominion over her own panic through the intellectual re-appropriation of objects, converting them into intellectual artifacts abstract enough to be prioritized, warranting gradations of alarm.

This the doe would have done. And stopped. Before bounding over the guardrail into traffic, stiffening in bloodless awe of the charging metal beast, which she would have dubbed *car*.

There's too much blood for perspective. The shattered glass. The dented curve of the hood, the roiling fresh smell of burning grass— or is it an earthy aroma, twigs and fecal matter, nuts and bone?

Edward makes sense of only a single hoof, which has reached in through the safety glass like a jagged pike. The animal's neck is broken across the frame which separates the passenger-side window and the windshield. An artery has been severed. Blood flows out in softening gushes down the vents, the radio, Jeanine's legs.

He reaches for Jeanine's knee before looking at her face. She's been thrown forward into the hoof. There's a gash in her neck, flowing, and she's slowly, almost absentmindedly, dabbing it with her fingers as if she's feeling for a blemish. A cut over her forehead turns her tilted ear into a small bowl for blood.

His head aching furiously, Edward scrambles from the car and heaves the hot deer from the hood. The body is heavy and comes away with a tearing sound, slumping slowly against the fender.

Edward slides back into the driver's seat, finds a chamois in the footwell. He presses it against the wound in Jeanine's neck.

"Can you hold it there?" He keeps searching, but sees no cars.

She nods weakly.

"Keep it pressed tight," he says.

The center of the rag blurs into a raspberry-colored blotch.

"Stick with me," he says.

And were Edward given the gift of elevated awareness, like that granted a deer who knows her own name, he might, in that moment, discern a ticklish double entendre: stick with me. The tacky blood sticking her clothes to her skin, but more importantly the long-range implications: stick with me—stay with me forever, be my wife, my lover, give me children, press your elderly and enfeebled hands in mine on our fortieth wedding anniversary and thank the good Lord as our children and grandchildren cheer our life together.

Stick with me.

Truth be told, he's waited so long for someone to come along, he can't fathom it not happening. When he was a young man, he used to wonder what was wrong. Why hadn't he met someone? He spoke slowly, yes, and women seemed to find him funny in an unflattering way. He kept a dog for a little while, and the dog was loyal. Its name was Cody. But Cody barked and barked all day long, when Edward was at work, and the neighbors complained, and he gave Cody to his nephew, who swore he knew how to "dog whisper." A year later, Cody had disappeared. When Edward came to visit, he was too polite to ask what had happened.

*

At this speed, the car bucks and wobbles, cresting hill after hill. No exit. No town. No hospital. But a fog has begun churning in Edward's mind. Why would he need a hospital? He's forgetting. There's a knot over his right eye that's begun to swell; his head must have struck the steering wheel. He touches it lightly and slows. No hurry, no worry, he thinks. He tries to reassemble the scrambled pieces of his brain. He gets the sense he's forgotten something. A white web of pirouetting sunlight appears in the fissured glass.

"You'll be my breath should I grow old," he sings softly.

He's thinking of their life together, he and Jeanine, as she sleeps beside him on their first vacation.

Truth be told, she found out she was pretty a long time ago. When she was fifteen, men stopped being able to hear her. It was as if she were speaking in a dog-whistle voice. Average ears didn't register her questions about biology, about menu items, about lumber for her patio or the life expectancy of tires.

"This is a man's world," James Brown sang on the radio. And Jeanine sang along to that with a hallelujah-hand held high over the steering wheel as she drove. She thought about buying a dog, someone who'd listen, but still couldn't bring herself to take on that responsibility.

The house overlooks the beach and sits on beams that raise it above high water. Edward pulls into the carport below.

"I'll take our things up," he says. His speech is slurry and garbled. "Why don't you go down to the shore." He opens the trunk and hauls out the luggage. He totes it all up to the bedroom and descends again to find Jeanine still sitting in the car. The bloody rag is stuck to her neck. She's staring blankly out the obliterated window with eyes filmed over.

"I thought you were going to the beach," he says.

He's still having trouble with his mind. The gnarl of sexual anticipation inside his stomach has petrified. He lowers his head to hers. Her breathing has the same rhythm as the waves breaking along the shore.

There's still time, he thinks. For incomparable sex and a life together. He refuses to hear otherwise.

"Still time to get to know you," he says.

Truth be told, when she was only five, a neighbor boy, home from college, babysat her and her sister. Her sister was three. He drove them to the beach—they lived in St. Augustine then—and the world was hot, the aching summer practically blistering the leather seats in the car so that she and her sister were forced to tuck their dresses beneath their legs.

The boy told them they were on an adventure. They parked at the seaside and he cracked the windows. Then he left them there. Jeanine could see him beyond the hood of the car meeting his summer fling, a long-legged girl with dark brown hair down to her denim shorts. The two of them pawed at one another in the shadow of a deserted pier while Jeanine and her sister surveyed the sand and the ocean and the rising surf washing its white into the beach. It got very, very hot. Her sister stuck out her tongue to express how dry it was. Jeanine took her hand and told her all they had to do was to wait and not get in trouble.

Another car pulled alongside them. Jeanine and her sister hid. After the people got out, she rose up and looked into the other car to see a small terrier staring back at her.

The terrier began to bark. Jeanine barked back. She made a game of it, testing the cadences, the ferocity, the pitch, to determine the dog's language. The dog heard her her and seemed to understand. They barked at one another for a very long time until the college boy came back.

By then her sister was dead of heat stroke.

That's what this feeling is like. The heat making her brain a woozy mess. The man is speaking to her, but he's lost sight of reality. He's slipped. He's apparently, reverted to his own desire. He's whispering about her joining him in the ocean, about finally, the two of them consummating—he's using that word. He's talking about grandchildren. The air has cooled, and her eyes have gone dry from being open too long. Blood has congealed down her shirt.

She remembers only the impact. But now—well—

Sweet Jesus, I need to make this happen myself, she thinks. I need to make my voice goddamn-well heard for the first time in my life.

Or something like it. Her thoughts have lost the shapeliness of words. She's become an entity of instinct. She has an unabating desire for survival. On some level, she knows the man has turned her into something carelessly remade out of his own need, like many men before. She's never felt this weak.

The sun drops behind them as he carries her to the ocean. A chill comes over her as the saltwater soaks her shorts, her shirt, caresses her stomach in a fine wash of foam. The water fills her mouth. She heaves a tiny sputter to keep from drowning in it.

He kisses her cheek. A part of her doesn't blame him. He strikes her as needy—*in need*. Maybe he thinks he can love her, and she him. But love, as a large thing with a span of decades, is too elusive. Love to her now, truth be told, would be a simple moment of rescue, a rush of relief from the oppressive heat.

He's whispering to her now. He seems to recognize the fact that he's committed an error. He's scared and loosening his grip.

"I'm sorry," he says. "I'm sorry."

She feels him letting go.

If the ocean were aware of the people near it, it might occasionally manifest a helping wave. It might gently spritz the young lovers on the beach in a cold shower that sends them trundling back to the car, their senses regained, to save two neglected children from the heat.

The ocean might recognize one man, dazed and acting out of his own shock, carrying a near-dead woman into its watery embrace. The ocean would glean this man's desperation, his need for love, his act a hopelessly and idiotically romantic gesture garnered from his muddled ideas about love's cruelty. The ocean would slap him with a flat, cold swell. It would show him the woman's shallow breathing, her unvanquished life clinging to the night air. It would save her.

It would save him.

But, truth be told, the ocean is not aware, the college boy was not aware, the deer was not aware, and Edward, in his holy thrall of the what-could-be, has never been aware, has in fact been so blind with desire as to never see Jeanine at all.

You can't count on any of them, she thinks. And before the last wave can shove its way into her nostrils, she summons her hand to rise from the water, to clutch the man's hair and bend him to her.

He looks stunned, she thinks, to be pulled this way, and he responds slowly by puckering his lips toward hers. But she yanks his head to the side so she's speaking into his ear. She forces the words from her mouth.

See me, she says. It's the unpardonable language of hope, a command that might have saved her sister, the deer, and the dog.

See me, she says.

See me. See me. See me.

KAPOK

SHE HAD READ IN *NATIONAL GEOGRAPHIC* THAT SOMEWHERE in South America near the heart of the Amazon River basin, along the quaggy mudbank of the Madeira, stands a Kapok tree, a ghost-white immensity one-hundred-and-fifty-feet tall with roots that flow from its base like ossified magma forming spider-leg tendrils. Stretching out to mingle with lianas and extend into ant-riddled devil's gardens, this tree buries its appendages into the histosolic soil like so many ostrich heads. Given the complexity, the absolute ultimateness of such a tree, one might be forgiven if—being so close to its ragged seed bundles, its ruby-petaled flowers, and its trunk of thorns along the outward-flowing radicles—one were to forget that the rest of the jungle existed. In other words, if one missed the forest for the tree.

This is what it was like to live with someone, Anne thought. The quirkily knotted boughs of a life carried out in close proximity often obscured the broader picture. But now that she'd had time to think, weren't there a thousand things she'd missed?

Exhibit A: the man standing in front of her in the checkout line, mid-afternoon, the two of them surrounded by bubble gum, breath mints, assorted candies with crudely bright lettering, and thumbed-through tabloids hastily jammed back into their stands.

He stood six feet tall in hand-stitched shoes, neatly tailored tweed suit, a fresh haircut, silk blue tie. A looker. A breathtaking man with a clean jaw, a nose only slightly too large for his cheeks, which gave him an air of sincerity. Handsome didn't do him justice. He looked healthy, upright, upstanding, kind, yet mysterious.

It wasn't until Anne noticed his eyes that she realized he'd once been her husband.

On the drive home through Cincinnati's Friday-evening traffic to her colorless suburb and her unilluminated house, she called

Jeanine. Jeanine showed up just as Anne was trying to remember where she put produce.

She held aloft a bag of tomatoes. "Where do you keep these at your house?"

"I leave them in the garden until I'm ready."

Jeanine smiled, and for a moment Anne hated her. Jeanine looked the gorgeous forty she was. Her hair was a natural blonde, her hands so expressive they seemed dissociated from the rest of her. She glowed with a kind of hippie vibe, a Stevie Nicks mashup with Jane Fonda. Anne's sensible, shoulder-length haircut and Gap-centric wardrobe, by comparison, were the mark of a middle class oppressed by mediocrity, doomed to die the neatly packaged life of shut-ins.

"Forget it," Anne said. "I saw Ranger, is all."

"Ranger?" Jeanine's hands fluttered. "Really? How was he?"

"I didn't 'engage' him. He looked terrific. He looked—God—like a different human being."

"Might have been. Just someone *similar* to Ranger."

"It was him."

"But you didn't say hello?"

"It's been over three years, and he looked good. Not just good, but good-good. He looked expensive. The old Ranger—*my* husband—used to spend Saturdays on the couch, all football season, eating nachos from Taco Bell. He was a slob, for one thing. When we were first married, I had to convince him it wasn't okay to piss in the shower."

"That's men," Jeanine said. "Heathens. Right?"

"How do I make this clear? The *version* of Ranger Davis I saw in the grocery store today should have been on the front of *GQ*. He was George Clooney, or pick whoever, someone suave and genteel."

"And you think this reflects negatively on yourself."

"The facts have spoken." Anne held up a finger to signal a point. "One: a man is with me twelve years. Two: during that twelve years he works as a teacher of fifth grade children. Three: he joins a bowling team. Four: he develops a fantasy football addiction for which we go to counseling—once. And five: he cultivates a set of love handles and a beer gut."

"His gut wasn't that bad," Jeanine said. "You're dwelling on the negatives. He treated you nice. He didn't cheat. You took vacations."

"After the divorce, I kept asking myself, did he love me? We met the summer after law school. We married, we set the TiVo, we watched our shows. We didn't have kids. Then he left."

"Is that what this is?" Jeanine squinted as if trying to read something in small print on Anne's forehead. "Some pity party you don't have a family? Because we had this conversation. Age twenty-three. You chose."

"What the hell does twenty-three know? Law school. DA's office. Glamor and good-doing. That's it. I'm in for life. I haven't had a promotion in six years."

"That's the economy. You just never moved on. You need to forget about Ranger."

"Do you know what I've been thinking all evening? No way that man still teaches fifth grade. No way those clothes are an affectation. Being healthy, trim. That's not a mid-life crisis. It's deep change, and it's facilitated by a whole other lifestyle."

Jeanine leaned on the counter. "A whole other life, huh? Maybe that's your answer. Maybe he's a secret agent. Maybe when he was with you, he was undercover, and now he's back to the world of international espionage."

Anne set the tomatoes down on the counter and rolled one beneath her palm. "A secret agent," she said.

Had Ranger seen her? Pretended not to? Or—and this was egregiously worse—had she become so plain and old-looking that this man, who she'd shared her life with, hadn't noticed her a few feet away?

She became obsessed, stewed about it for weeks, and ultimately looped back around to Jeanine's proposition: Ranger, the spy.

Was it so ridiculous? The explanation would cleanly kill the two proverbial birds with one stone: if Ranger were a spy, 1) he wouldn't be able to acknowledge her presence in the grocery store without blowing his cover, and 2) it might account for the sudden breakup of their marriage.

Just to be clear, the spy-theory wasn't entirely out of the blue. There was evidence to support it. There'd been the time she and Ranger were sitting at a stoplight in Clifton. On their way home from a party, she was driving, and Ranger was sitting in the passenger seat with his window rolled down to the warm night air. From the shadows, like in a movie, a thin man emerged and raised a revolver, pointing it through the open window.

"Get out and give me the car," he said.

Time didn't slow down, like some people say, but the charge of adrenaline honed Anne's perceptions to certain details. The man's voice was too high, for instance, pinched, pre-pubescent-sounding, though he looked sixty. His face was a blur of gray stubble. Michael Jackson's "The Way You Make Me Feel" was playing so softly on the radio that only Michael's *hee-hees* and *come-on-girls!* were audible. All observations as helpful in surviving a carjacking as a gazelle admiring the sway of prairie grass during a lion attack.

The man wiggled the pistol. "I said, get out. I'm taking your car."

Ranger looked up and said, "Not tonight, bud. Sorry." He turned to Anne. "Drive," he said calmly. "Run the red light. There's no one coming."

She pressed down on the gas, drove through the intersection, feeling the incongruous and illicit thrill of breaking the law. The man with the gun didn't fire or give chase. The radio moved on to other eighties hits, a theme for the evening's programming. As she pulled into the garage, the door sliding down behind them, she began to weep.

"God, I thought we were going to die," she said.

"We could have," he replied.

And for years she was angry he'd said that. She'd wanted him to tell her there'd been no danger—that, through some trick of the light, he'd noticed there were no bullets in the cylinder. Instead he'd suggested she take a slightly cold shower. That's the term he'd used: "slightly cold."

"To chill the panic," he said.

She didn't tell her parents about it for months. When they finally visited from Long Island and Ranger was out of the house, she let loose with everything, all the minutiae, including the part about Michael Jackson. Her mother was furious: "He could have got you killed." But her father nodded and said, "He's got a pair of balls on him, I'll give him that."

Ballsy, yes. But now, after seeing him in the grocery store, after Jeanine posited that absurd hypothesis, did it add up to something more? What if Ranger Davis had all along been a trained killer, a black-ops type, or whatever they called them? MI-6. CIA. NSA. What if in a moment like that, Ranger knew—with *absolute certainty*—he could have snapped that man's arm before the trigger was pulled?

On Saturday, she began a comprehensive search of her house. Any items that might shed light on Ranger's true identity. She looted the attic, then the basement, and the guest bedroom with its copious closet of winter clothes.

This yielded little.

Getting past the divorce had ultimately meant jettisoning Ranger's possessions. Particularly his t-shirts. For months she'd found these white cotton reminders hiding in every corner of the house. Behind the bed. Wadded up in the garage. Trunk of the car. Top of the refrigerator. She couldn't remember him removing them in these places. She couldn't remember stripping them off him in a fit of lovemaking or him peeling them away after mowing the lawn. They were just there. No matter where she found them, they smelled like Ranger, his skin, his deodorant, his soap, even his sweat, that acrid aroma which had somehow developed a kind of nostalgic sweetness. In the name of reclaiming a little dignity, she'd thrown them all out.

Because life, post-divorce, had not been so much an easing into the serene waters of a new Anne as an overly long epilogue recounting the old one. The thing she'd discovered was that divorce, unlike other forms of trauma, was too common for sympathy. People didn't care. Divorce wasn't interesting or uplifting in any of the right ways. Sometimes it didn't seem fair that Ranger hadn't been shot down over the Khyber Pass or kidnapped by FARC guerillas. At least then Anne might have had some reason for all those wasted evenings sobbing by the cold air return in the kitchen.

Ultimately though, she'd moved on, not only by disposing of Ranger's t-shirts, but by discarding everything. The last hurdle had been the wedding ring. She'd carried it in her pocket because wearing it on her finger would have looked too pathetic. But she rolled it between her fingers during meetings. She slipped it on and off in the darkness of a theater as she watched the leading woman and her beau overcome the point of contention that had kept them apart for the past ninety minutes. Pathetic. Then, on a Wednesday afternoon, she arrived home from work and hauled the trash to the curb. It was dusk. She scanned the neighborhood. Not another human being in sight. She'd had court that day and was still wearing a pants suit with a blazer with an inner pocket. The ring was there. She pulled it out and looked it over in the dying light, a little piece of metal, unadorned and simple. Its closeness to her body had kept it warm. It felt like nothing. She dropped it into the trashcan and walked back to the house.

After that, she started to feel like her own person. Encountering an old classmate on the street a month later, she'd gone so far as to brag about getting her life back. She referred to herself as a "singular and unencumbered entity." The other woman had touched Anne's shoulder, given her a tight-lipped smile, and said, "Good for you."

Looking back, maybe the classmate had been right to look skeptical. After all Anne's steps to regain her individuality, there was still a confounded sense of loss, a stupefied and bewildered search for some reason as to why her marriage had ended. She didn't really know. Not unless, that is, Ranger were a spy.

She found little in the house to confirm this hypothesis. What leftover possessions of Ranger's she did find were without meaning. She even took apart a ballpoint pen to see if it had a listening device inside. It did not. Only blue ink that ruined her shirt.

By mid-week she cleared the last of her work, re-routed certain cases, and put in a request for all three weeks of her vacation.

The following Monday, she crouched in her Camry at Trader Joe's. Eight in the morning until nine at night. In that time, she managed to read one hundred pages of *The Count of Monte Cristo*, achieve a high score on CandyCrush, and to sunburn her left arm.

No Ranger.

She called Jeanine on her way home. Jeanine brought over a bottle of wine.

"I didn't think you'd go through with it," Jeanine said. "I honestly didn't."

"I have no contact information. Nothing. He quit his job, and I've searched the internet—the entire thing. He's not there except for some old stuff about a spring social."

"You can't tell me that during all the divorce proceedings you didn't have his number."

Jeanine hadn't been around during the split. She'd been hiking in Nepal or doing something vaguely spiritual. There'd been a man who wrote for *Outside* magazine. Jeanine had brought him by for drinks before they left the country together. The only thing Anne remembered about the man was that he'd lost his pinky while rappelling. He'd shown her the nub and told her, for the sake of continuing to mountain climb, that he strengthened the nub by kneading silly putty. The whole day, whether it was traveling or sitting at his desk, he worked that wad of silly putty over and over with his half-pinky.

Jeanine didn't return from Nepal for almost two years, and when she did, it was without the magazine writer. Anne met her at the airport, still reeling from the divorce. Near the baggage claim they held one another, and Anne whispered, "Did he ever love me?"

Jeanine said, "It doesn't matter, does it?" And since then, the two of them had acted like it didn't. They talked little of Ranger, never of the divorce. Jeanine refused. So Anne was more than a little surprised it was coming up now.

Anne smeared a bright green blob of aloe on her arm. "During the divorce, I could reach him. But once we settled, he switched his number."

"No strings attached?"

"He wrote up a list of minor grievances attesting to the necessity of the divorce. Mundane stuff. I didn't fight it. I just didn't have an argument for why we *shouldn't* part ways. Afterward, I hated myself for letting it happen."

"Bit extreme, though. Cutting off all contact."

"But what was I supposed to do? The week after we signed the papers, I found thirty pair of his dress socks in the linen closet. I figured he'd packed them up and forgot. I tried to call, be reasonable, but the phone didn't ring. That was it."

Jeanine touched Anne's forearm. "I feel like I've thrown you a psychic red herring."

"You're talking about the spy thing."

"You know I was just kidding, right?"

Anne frosted her shoulder with a second layer of aloe. "I don't know anymore."

In a long-sleeve t-shirt, Anne stared at the storefront of the grocery store. Banners touting salmon and bananas blocked a clear view of the registers. At least she'd parked more strategically today. The morning sun was hitting the passenger side, giving her tender arm a break. A small shade tree, planted to her left, would block the afternoon rays.

A yellow legal pad sat in her lap. At the top she'd written, *EVIDENCE.* Her trusty, gold-trimmed Mont Blanc, which she'd received as a gift from her father for graduating law school, rested placidly atop it.

Thinking of her father now, it was no wonder she'd chosen Ranger Davis as a husband. Her father had said fewer words to her in her teens than he had to the mailman. In college, it hadn't been much better, their three-second phone conversations mere formalities before her mother picked up the receiver. The pen was maybe what constituted a grand gesture for a retired math teacher, meant to overcome all that silence.

Ranger had possessed her father's demeanor. Quiet. Steady. Somewhat unaffectionate, at least in public. To strangers he came off unemotional and calculating, which Anne had taken, in a kinder light, for being reserved, even timid.

"Slightly cold," she thought now. A man with hidden agendas. But was he a spy, or did he love her? The two were incompatible.

On the legal pad, evidence mounted quickly.

One: a barbecue at Anne's boss's house when a woman from her office dropped a plate. Ranger dipped down and caught it. Granted, a pickle had been lost, but he'd saved the hamburger. Do normal people have reflexes like that?

Two: The vacation on a beach in North Carolina, early in their marriage. Ranger and Anne's brother, Jack, swam out to sea, an overly macho game of chicken to test who was willing to go further. Ranger kept paddling until he was out of sight, his head lost in the rank and file of waves. When Jack came into shore, panting, his long arms limp as noodles, there'd been ten minutes—what felt like days—before Ranger returned, sliding up out of the churned white surf, his brown muscles taut, bouncing on the balls of his toes as he jogged lightly up the sand and plunked himself down on the towel. It seemed to hint at some inner power unbeknownst to her.

Addended to this item, she wrote, *SPECIAL NAVY TRAINING?*

Three: The carjacking.

Four: A few years into their marriage she'd found five trashbags full of mundane-looking documents in the garage. When she asked him what they were, he told her they were from the school. He'd offered to recycle them since there was no program to do so at the elementary. But he'd also insisted, legally, he had to shred the papers first. He spent an entire evening doing just that while listening to a Reds game.

Lesser instances followed, all with possibly underlying motives.

She started a second column. Proof he'd loved her. She was digging for the big-money gesture, some equivalent to her father gifting her the pen. What had Ranger done, she thought, to demonstrate his affection and devotion?

This was harder. Barring basic Valentine's cards, birthday

dinners, and lovemaking on particular occasions (sex in the backyard while the city's Fourth-of-July fireworks bloomed overhead), no distinct proof he'd really loved her existed. How do twelve years go by without a single highlight?

She'd finished Point Eighteen in the spy column when her passenger door swung open and Jeanine slid in.

"Holy shit, you scared me."

"You thought I was Ranger maybe?" Jeanine said. "Stop and think: if your ex-husband really is a spy, the one thing he'd most certainly be able to do is recognize a woman—his ex-wife no less—surveilling him from a car in a half-empty parking lot."

Anne rested the pen on the page. Her obsession seemed suddenly as ridiculous as it was.

"You're the lawyer," Jeanine said. "You should see the paradox. If you try to prove Ranger is a spy by waiting for him to show up, then by showing up, he's probably not a spy. But, if he is a spy, then he probably won't show up again."

"Am I really as stupid as this makes me sound?"

Jeanine pulled a bag of pistachios from her sequin-flowered purse. "We're blinded by our loves and obsessions."

"Eastern proverb?"

"An inevitability. I realized, despite you being crazy as a loon for doing this, my real duty as a friend is to sit with you. See you through the fever." She saluted. "I'm in it for the long haul."

Anne and Jeanine waited sixteen days. Jeanine, who owned a clothing store and employed two moody but apparently trustworthy twenty-somethings, left only in the evenings to count the till. Otherwise she was there beside Anne. Sometimes they talked. Sometimes they didn't. Sometimes they switched sides to ensure they received even exposure to the sun. It was all lackluster and somehow subtly thrilling.

Then on the seventeenth day, late in the afternoon, Ranger Davis stepped into the grocery store.

"He does look good," Jeanine said.

A few message boards dedicated to private investigation recommended a tailing distance of between fifty to seventy yards, preferably in medium traffic. They waited for him to leave, then pulled out onto 275 and hung back from his Jaguar, an opal-colored vehicle, slim as a fish, with fine slices of chrome accenting its body. Not the vehicle of a fifth-grade teacher any more than his wardrobe was that of a man who got stuck with playground duty.

"This is so much fun," Jeanine cooed.

They exited the highway and traveled east until the urban sprawl fell away. The landscape greened, growing silent and subdued. Forests on either side filled with lightning bugs. The road transformed into a winding rural ribbon of escalatingly expensive houses with gated driveways, callboxes built into stone pillars, and addresses marked by bronze plaques.

"Ritzy neighborhood," Jeanine said.

A minute later, Ranger's Jaguar suddenly accelerated, rounded a tight curve, and winked out of sight. Anne's heart surged. Her hands involuntarily tightened around the wheel.

"Keep driving," Jeanine said. "Doesn't mean he saw us."

Anne took the bend.

Standing beside the road with his arms crossed, leaning against his parked car, stood Ranger.

They zipped by and he fell out of sight.

"What do we do?" Jeanine said.

"He saw us."

"Obviously he saw us."

"Did he recognize us?" Anne said.

"He's your husband."

"He recognized us. He had that look."

"Turn around, is what I say. Face him. Fess up."

"We'd sound ridiculous."

"More ridiculous than doing a drive-by sighting?"

Anne felt the blood running out of her face. Now she thought about it, she didn't care to see Ranger's new life. A big part of her could accept the spy theory and leave it alone.

"What if we blow his cover?" she said.

"Stop."

"I'm serious. If he's a spy, we might be mucking up an important assignment."

"No. I mean, stop. I'm driving."

Anne parked. Jeanine took command of the wheel. By the time they'd turned around, Ranger was gone. The gate stood open behind him.

"We shouldn't do this," Anne said.

Jeanine mashed the pedal, her sweet and natural smile unwavering as they puttered up the winding drive through the woods.

The house occupied the top of a hill like a sentinel. The sky opened up in a darkening blue, stark above the roof through the aperture of manicured trees, highlighting the house's imposing presence. Strictly speaking, it was a single-story home, though single-story in the massive and imposing way of museums or institutions. Sprawling and vast, it was a cross between a Malibu beach house and Angkor Wat. Thousands of six-inch-square blocks, carved with bas-relief symbols of island gods or arcane runes from Celtic cultures, made up its front wall. Interspersed throughout the blocks were hundreds of small windows that made a glowing yellow pattern that stood out under the crush of dusk.

"What the hell is this place?" Anne said.

"Scientology, I bet," Jeanine said. "We're in L. Ron Hubbard territory."

They parked and stood by the car, waiting for whatever security was about to swoop down. Instead, Ranger opened the red front door, drink in hand. He waved them to enter.

"Come in," he said. "It's good to see you both."

Jeanine took Anne's hand as they approached. Stepping silently inside, Anne waited for Jeanine to conjure up a good excuse for their presence. But Jeanine was staring at the tall ceilings, the copious room stretching at least a hundred feet to the back wall.

Anne peered across the designer leather furniture at the eclectic art—impressionist paintings, a delicate bronze sculpture, aboriginal works, a small Lichtenstein (the only thing Anne could identify).

"You've certainly done well for yourself," Jeanine said.

"We do okay," he said.

Anne's ears burned with that "*WE.*"

He poured them drinks as if he'd been expecting them. He'd remembered Anne's affinity for Manhattans, Jeanine's preference for Sauvignon Blanc, which had already been chilled. He bid them sit and they did. Anne thought about Ranger always controlling the situation, the way he'd commanded her to drive away from the gunman, the way he'd told her to take a shower, 'slightly cold.'

He refilled his own drink and seated himself. "To what do I owe the pleasure?"

"We followed you," Anne blurted.

"Of course you did. What I mean is, How can I be of service?"

Of service? Had he ever spoken this way?

"All right," Jeanine said. "What happened is we saw you today at the grocery store. We tried to get your attention, but you must not have heard us in the parking lot." She laughed, a floaty sort of giggle, making it sound as natural as it could. "So—and this is my fault—I made Anne follow you. Crazy, I know. But she has a question for you. It's been irritating her, I think, and as a friend, I couldn't let that itch continue."

Anne realized Jeanine had left open the possibility for a real question, not one about espionage.

Ranger stared at her. "A question?"

Anne set down her drink. "Why did you cut off all contact? Was I really that bad? I mean, didn't you love me?"

It felt good asking. She'd even begun to breathe more regularly, but just then a man, a smidge taller than Ranger, entered the room from the open kitchen. His temples were graying, and he had a trim, black moustache. He wore a polo shirt and white tennis shorts.

"Oh," he said. "Guests. Staying for dinner?"

Ranger stood and held out an arm as if presenting the man to a crowd. "Ladies, this is Timothy. Timothy, this is Anne and Jeanine, my ex-wife and her friend."

Timothy smiled brightly. "The elusive Anne," he said. "I've heard a thing or two about you."

"I haven't," Anne said.

"Well," Timothy said, "that goes with the territory, I assume."

"I don't get it," Anne said. "I don't get any of it."

"You look pale as a geisha," Jeanine said.

"Please," Ranger said, "have a seat. We'll chat a bit more, and you girls can stay for dinner."

Anne slouched back into a seated position, her posterior resting on what might be the couch, but she wouldn't have sworn to it. The room was evaporating, darkening, then pulsing back to life around her. She didn't understand where she was or the rules of whatever was happening right now. She'd never once been able to pinpoint why Ranger left, or how the life they'd created could have been anything other than what it was. Certainly Ranger now, in his tailored shirt, his Ferragamo tie, sitting on a couch that probably cost more than her car, with a strange man smiling in her direction like a kindly and affluent uncle, had proven that another life did exist, one parallel and quite possibly better than the one he'd been leading with her.

This left one logical conclusion: she'd been the one keeping him from something, a fulfillment multi-planar, blurred like an open horizon with the sheer magnitude of sumptuous possibilities. Her heart ached to think so. But if that were the case, she wanted him to say it.

"Please," she said, "what happened?"

Jeanine placed a hand on Anne's forearm. "Maybe it's time to go."

"Did you win the lottery?" Anne said.

He laughed. "No. And no inheritance. Nothing hidden away when we parted."

Anne didn't know what to say about that, and so sat there silently. The conversation congealed into a gelatinous, cold pile of pudding. Timothy rose and made himself a drink, a sidecar. A wedge of blood orange was perched on the lip of the cocktail glass. The uncommon hue of the orange made Anne feel as if reality had been skewed.

"So what is it?" Jeanine said. "Anne obviously isn't going to ask, so I will. What are you doing here?"

"I'm having a drink," he said, "with old friends."

"Is that what we are? Because it seems like you intended never to see us again."

"I had other plans."

"New career?"

Anne turned to Jeanine. "Quit giving him the third degree. He doesn't have to answer." She looked at Ranger. "It just hurts. I want you to know, you hurt me. Until now, I don't think I realized how much."

"I never meant that to be the case," he said.

"Maybe we should go," Jeanine said again. "Things are a certain way. We don't have to ask any more questions."

But Anne hadn't let go, hadn't yet climbed out of her own shock. "We thought you might be a spy," she said.

Jeanine let out a half-silent, "No, don't."

"We thought you might be one of those button-down, suburban operatives who claims a business trip one weekend, then flies to Fallujah for an extraction of foreign nobility."

"I don't know that he needs to hear any of this," Jeanine said.

"An 'operative'? Like James Bond?"

Anne felt defensive—"It's not that crazy."

Ranger turned to Timothy and flipped his palm toward the ceiling in a see-what-I-mean kind of gesture. "Be clear, Annie,"—he'd called her that, Annie, when they inhabited some uncomplicated version of their life before the divorce—"you thought, or even think now, that I was a spy, and all that time teaching grade school, I what?"

Seized lungs, constricted throat, cramping stomach. Through an onslaught of defiant bodily afflictions, she forced a squeaky little reply: "Yes. I don't know the details, but yes. A spy."

Because if not a spy, if not a spy—then what? The forest for the trees, she thought. Something she hadn't seen by dint of the close-up, the overly intimate quarters of matrimony. She'd missed something.

Jeanine let out a little moan and moved her hand up Anne's shoulder. "Come on," she said.

Anne became aware of her hands in her lap. The room had turned into a still life, a blotted acrylic of immoveable and unfathomable set pieces. Life had slowed to the point of motionless suffering. Anne's life. But she resisted Jeanine's plea to go. A minute ticked by. Another, the four of them sinking into silence. She didn't know what face she was making, but it must have been something pained, all too reflective of the way she felt, because Ranger's polite smile slid away from his mouth.

It seemed it might go on this way forever, but then Ranger, as only Ranger could, with a single motion, set the still room spinning again.

He leaned forward, growing somber, almost grim. "Don't say anything more. I sweep for bugs, but you can never be too careful."

He lowered his voice. "My life with you was the assignment."

"I don't understand," Anne whispered.

"Deep cover. Twelve years."

"You were a school teacher."

He signaled for her to lower her voice. "Look, it's all very complicated. Do you know what F-1 visas are?" He rose and sat beside her on the couch. "Ordinary student visas. Foreign students aren't covered by our taxes. The money has to come from somewhere, usually foreign corporations, groups, or families paying for the education. Thousands of sources, and it turns out a huge percentage of them after 9/11 were overpaying."

"Extra money coming into the country," Jeanine said. Anne felt Jeanine against her shoulder, leaning in.

"That's right. Extra money siphoned off over thousands of school districts and collected in a central location. Ohio."

Timothy stood and a little ostentatiously set down his drink. "Ranger, you can't. You're jeopardizing the mission." His hand went to his forehead, his teeth clenched. "Think of our cover."

Ranger waved him off. "Our sleepy, little school was a model district for a nationwide campaign to normalize all exchange programs. As such, it received federal funding, and all the records for those thousands of other programs came back to our central office. Took me years, but I tracked tens of thousands of transactions to a single source, middle-eastern in origin."

"Al-Qaeda?" Anne said. The word dribbled out in a whisper.

Ranger leaned back. "I've said too much."

"You've said too much!" Timothy repeated.

They stared quietly, absorbing this information. Ranger's phone rang. He answered and walked briskly toward the kitchen, talking loudly.

"Yes," he said. "Two Jehovah's Witnesses. Yes. I'll get rid of them." He hung up. "You have to go. If you ever need me, put a handwritten note in my mailbox. Don't sign it."

He led them to the front door. Anne's heart was beating so fast. It was like the night with the gunman. She didn't know what to pay attention to. She kept looking at Ranger, at Timothy, searching the corners of the house for spy-type cameras or tiny microphones in the stonework, then Ranger's eyes, the way his mouth was not smiling, but not unsmiling, rather sure and comforting.

"Why tell me now?" she said. "Why, after all this time, tell me about your mission?"

"Because it's over," he said. He didn't elaborate.

"We're going to have to lie low!" Timothy stage-whispered behind them. They moved through the door.

"Act natural as you go," Ranger whispered.

Jeanine hustled toward the car, goading Anne to hurry. Ranger stood in the doorway, watching them, waving as if it were any other day. Playing it cool to the last.

As they reached the bottom of the drive, Jeanine let out a long breath and stared at Anne like she was watching a grenade with its pin removed. Anne peered back through the window. The house on the hill had become a sliver of roof wedged between the trees, a dark and miniscule spot she wouldn't have recognized as a structure if she didn't already know it.

Had he loved her? Or was he a spy? The questions circled one another like prizefighters in a ring.

She thought of the pen her father had given her—substantive evidence he'd loved her. Jeanine's time spent staking out the grocery store—more evidence.

And Ranger.

Ranger telling her.

Finally telling her—those prizefighters embracing—he'd loved her.

Loved her *and* a spy.

She remembered now the time in the kitchen, the two of them dancing wildly to Fine Young Cannibals on the radio, beaming madly as they jigged around the pizza she'd just dropped. The pizza had landed face down on the tile floor, but he'd mended the moment, set her dancing when the ruined meal had seemed to her like the end of the world. The walk through the cactus garden at Christmas in Nevada, his arm hooked about her waist, the two of them flowing like water in the desert, in step, working their way about the park full of children, talking of their own, their own one day, one day their own children. His constant attempts at cooking scrambled eggs the way her mother used to do, his failure, so that no matter what he did, the eggs were never the same as when she was a little girl, and she never told him so, about the something still missing. And finally the retreat, the bid for deliverance, a whole week he was away to renew the passion he'd forgotten when their bodies pressed together, his iteration and assertion of rejuvenated affections upon his return before it all fell apart. How had she forgotten that? That he'd tried. That he'd given her every plausibility for a cover story, and she hadn't taken it.

Maybe this spoke poorly of her capacity for government fieldwork, but in her defense all she'd needed, the only thing she required, was his confession, because it was true—she hadn't seen the forest for the trees.

Ranger, the spy. Code Name: Kapok. It had a ring to it.

Driving home with Jeanine, she thought about this new and vital intelligence. I can live with that, she thought. Ranger, the spy, she thought.

Time to move on to other missions.

I THOUGHT OF YOU

I. *The Cost of Goat Cheese*

THE GLASS STOREFRONT TURNS THE PEOPLE ON THE STREET INTO ghosts. It's arid fall in New York. The gray sunshine is limitless, an ambient force that paints all objects, even the trees, the palatable and subdued hue of concrete. The air is neither chilly, hinting toward winter, nor the heavy-tongued heat of leftover summer that lingers in the asphalt of spider-veined alleyways. It's a nothing temperature.

In the storefront, I'm a translucent version of a thin man in his thirties wearing a light linen sport coat and an overly rumpled shirt. I'm a little too stoop-shouldered, posing on 38th Street as if I've been beamed into Midtown from an invisible mothership and am still trying to adjust to the Earth's gravity. This washed-out version of myself stares back at me, overlaid with the green letters of a catering company whose claim to fame is apparently that they serve chèvre with everything—sandwiches, fruit, croissants, the salmon salad wrap.

Next door to the caterer's is another business. Its entrance is set back into the building and hooded by a section of scaffolding that has been there as long as I've lived in the city. I've been through this door only once. Last time, less than a month ago, I bolted back out into the street after only a few seconds of standing and breathing the scent of cardamom, the burgundy zip of Aleppo, that nutty sweetness of pistachios, baklava, tomatoes, and whatever other homecooked foods the proprietor, Amin, unabashedly cooks on a series of hot plates and crockpots, which he keeps perched on low stools and plugged into wall outlets behind the counters. He's a man of distinct tastes, Amin. I'm told he's Syrian but won't claim it when he's asked directly. He's said to have a daughter he's disowned who still lives near Beirut and serves as one of the "lionesses of al-Assad," a female militia group protecting the president. But all of this is speculation.

The food, which Amin is known to offer his clients, is not his trade. Only a passionate hobby that keeps him occupied throughout the day as he waits for customers, many of them unhappy men like myself, to enter the shop and sheepishly hem and haw until he catches their meaning and smiles beneath his neatly trimmed moustache. Amin has a calming smile, I'm told, and can make anyone feel at ease about the most desperate circumstances.

I enter Amin's shop and begin counting. If I make it to ten, I'll be okay.

The room is cramped, about twenty by twenty, with unadorned walls, a patchy custard-colored paint job. There's a U-shaped counter running the length of all three walls. From the layout, the place looks to have once been a jewelry store. Amin continuously patrols the area behind this counter, lifting a crockpot lid and occasionally releasing a heavily scented puff of steam that wafts to the ceiling like an escaped soul.

I reach ten. I realize I've been counting on my fingers. My left pinky slowly extends and I breathe the air more deeply. Amin hasn't acknowledged my presence. I finally approach and clear my throat in a fake cough. He's slow to turn, only doing so after using his sleeve to clean the little window on an automatic breadmaker. He watches the goings-on inside. The little machine makes a resolute and rhythmic plodding noise that apparently makes Amin happy. He pats it like its a small child behaving especially well, then places his hands on the counter and says to me, "Now, how can I help you?"

His speech is surprisingly unaffected by either a Middle-Eastern lilt or a British bias. I immediately wonder if all I've been told about Amin is false, which makes me question my entire purpose for coming. It's possible I've been lied to on every front.

"I don't know," I say.

"You don't know how I can help you?"

"I don't," I say. "Not exactly. I mean, I have to find out if you can help."

"Oh," he says. "Let me put you at ease. I can. I can help."

"Are you sure? Do you know what I'm asking?"

"Do you?" he says. He holds out his hand. "Give it to me. Whatever it is."

I produce from my pocket a pair of women's underwear. They're striped horizontally in pink and black. He accepts them graciously.

"Are you married?" he says.

"No. I mean, I was. She passed away."

"And these are hers?"

"Yes."

"Good, good," he says. "Sometimes I receive things like this—they're from a lover, but the man is married. He's trying to be faithful, so he hopes to forget the other woman and the thrill of illicit sex. He brings me the lover's underthings. That's a tough kind of case because men like that—that's in their nature. You can't change a man's nature that way. You can change it, yes, but not like that."

"I don't want to change my nature," I say. "I just want to forget."

"Then you've been misinformed." He hands me back the underwear. "There is no forgetting. The human mind can hold all the events of one's life quite easily. This process isn't about forgetting."

"I've been misinformed," I repeat. "I'm sorry." I walk toward the door, but halfway there I stop. Despite the odds—the gray day, the narrow street, the high buildings, the scaffolding—a loving stream of sunlight has filtered its way down into this little room, coming to rest at my feet in a brilliant square that gives the tiles of Amin's floor an unnerving reality. If I step into that sunlight, I re-enter the world. I face the pain myself.

When I turn, he's smiling again.

"Just to be clear," I say, "how would this work if you're not going to make me forget?"

He waves me come closer. "Think of it this way. You can't forget anything. Nothing. Even the not-so-smart"—he taps his temple with his sturdy index finger—"are only covering." He sees I'm not understanding, so he starts again. He's a patient man, Amin. I've heard this, too.

"If memories are like furniture," he says, "in the vast room of our personal history, then we must accept that all the decor is permanent. The futon from our college years sits beside the crib of our infancy, which rests next to the hospital bed of our last days. This room of our history is also filled with lamps, coffee tables, et cetera et cetera et cetera." He smiles. "You get the joke?"

"I don't."

"*The King and I?* It was on Broadway for many years. Et cetera et cetera et cetera. Very much like my metaphor—and other things and other things and other things. Our memories pile up in our heads."

"The musical," I say.

"Or the film, sure. But Broadway. Broadway was the best. My point being that all of it continues to reside. Every new memory. Placed. Doesn't go away." Again he taps his temple. "So while we can't make you forget, we can change the memory. We can make it something else. Less like throwing one of these many couches out the window. More like covering it in a blanket. We change the couch itself to fit what we want. The ugly paisley pattern, gone. Re-upholstered in a rich green the color of shaded ferns. See?"

"No, I don't."

"Tell me about the underwear." He takes them again and holds them up. He avoids dangling them. Somehow they look dignified in his hand, rather than tawdry.

"I was told," I say, "that it was best, for the first item, to be something visceral. The more visceral the better. I brought my wife's underwear because these I remember. There was a Saturday morning in July. It was hot, and our air conditioning had been out for twenty-four hours. We had the windows in our apartment open, but there was no breeze. My wife had kicked off the covers in the night. The only thing she was wearing were these underwear. When I woke up she was lying there asleep, her legs apart, her arms flung out. I—"

I hesitate.

"Go on," he says. "I'm not here to write erotica. I don't get off on it."

"I woke her up gently. We made love. We were both sweaty and uncomfortable in the heat, but somehow the lovemaking was the best I ever had. We stayed in bed all day. There was nowhere to be, nothing to be done about the heat. We went to the kitchen for water. We came back. We did it again and again. It was all day."

"This is a very clear memory for you," he says.

"Yes."

"Good. And you're sure you want it to change?"

"I get sick," I say. "Just thinking about it now, I get sick. She's gone less than a year now, and it's only an ache." I point at the underwear. "I couldn't throw them away, but they're the worst thing I own. They're awful. I keep them in my sock drawer, and sometimes I see them and hurt so bad I have to sit on the bed and take deep breaths, ten minutes, fifteen, before I can move again."

He nods, places a hand over the underwear so they disappear.

"I'll sell them," he says. "Do me a favor. Go see a show. Go to Broadway. All this talk about *The King and I* has me nostalgic. I used to go to shows all the time. They were wonderful. I like the singing. I even like the chance something can go wrong."

He puts the underwear in the old jewelry display case. They're the only thing in there.

"Some pervert isn't going to get them, is he?"

"No no. I have a very strict policy. There is nothing like that. I screen very thoroughly. Now, go. Come back in a week."

I walk out into that gray sunshine wondering what I've done. I must be the most desperate sort of human being to trust my memory of Holly to the laughable and superstitious. I feel ashamed and hustle away into a dying afternoon, which grows colder by the minute.

II. *The Cost of Owning a Car*

Seven months ago, Holly died in a spat of heavy rain on Highway 95 just south of New Haven. She'd been on her way to Providence to see her sister, Rebecca. Around midnight, she entered a construction area and veered off the road, clipping a pylon and striking a tree. It appeared she'd hydroplaned.

Those are the details. The highlighted facts are utterly meaningless—a squashed construction barrel blaring orange in the headlights of a Connecticut State Police vehicle; a slender crag of white bisecting the center of the windshield where the impact rolled straight through the middle of the car like an awakened fault line; the spilled Werther's caramels on which Holly was snacking, their wrappers glittering gold in the footwell. The police came to my house. I confirmed her identity with a picture. After they left, I collapsed onto the kitchen floor and didn't move for two days. I pissed myself. At some point, I heard Rebecca pounding on the door. Her voice was small and sobbing. She went away.

On the third day, after getting no answer from me, my parents took a direct flight from Iowa City and let themselves in with a spare key. My mother wept over me. My father, still a powerful man, mustered his strength and carried me to the car as if I were a child again. I was admitted to Bellevue for malnutrition and dehydration. It was not lost on me that my parents had selected a facility also known for its psychiatric care.

I left the hospital. My parents returned reluctantly to their farm. I went back to my life, but didn't wholly recover. I carried out my workdays in a haze, stupefied by simple objects like staplers and copiers and swivelling chairs that had no right to exist if someone as radiant and incredible as Holly could be snuffed out like a dropped match on the water.

Rebecca began calling. We were both alone, both grieving. The first time we spoke, she made a little catching noise in the back of her throat. She said she was sorry about Holly.

"It's my fault," she said. "She was coming to see me."

"It's no one's fault."

She choked back a word and made a noise like a click on the line.

"What is it?" I said.

"I have to tell you," she said. "I have to." More of the clicking sound, a strangled little sob with no air behind it.

"Tell me what?"

Two, maybe three, times our conversations went this way until I stopped answering. I was sinking. After a week of avoiding Rebecca's calls, the first of her letters came in the mail. The envelope was a robin's-egg blue, like those for Easter cards or children's birthdays, except this one was the standard office size. In the upper lefthand corner was Rebecca's address in her almost stern little block letters.

I didn't open it. I placed it in an old shoebox and slid it under my bed to forget about it.

I continued on. The worst were the things left behind. The apartment, for months, was littered with emotional tripwires. I'd find something inconsequential—a tissue fallen behind the bedstand, wadded up in a particular way—and I'd know it was Holly's. I'd become incapacitated for hours. I'd sob, wail, beat my fists on the floor, sputter hopeless invectives, and on the worst nights finally pass out, awaking some time later, picking myself up, and hauling my racked body to bed before another day of work.

The problem seemed to be that Holly's things never lost their potency. Each item, no matter how ridiculous, had its own train of associations: moments shared, loving gestures, expressions with bottomless meaning. For my own safety, I gathered up these possessions, when I found them, and stowed them in the linen closet. I packed it into a single dense block with her things. After that, I avoided the closet at all costs. But I could still sense the objects behind the door every time I walked the hallway. I could feel them occupying their space, reminding me she was gone. My grief, rather than dissipating, threatened to flood every aspect of my life. I slept less. I wept sometimes till dawn.

At work, I stared at the coffeemaker, even when nothing was brewing. I'd get lost in some alternate history in which Holly survived. The dangerously addictive aspect of this daydreaming was that each time I did it, I conjured a vibrantly new scenario.

Sometimes Holly and I had children. Sometimes we bought a house in Vermont. Sometimes we changed careers. There were even visions in which some disaster befell us—a housefire or financial ruin—but each time we stuck it out together. It was the worst kind of fantasy, an impotent and misplaced hope leaving me exhausted and useless for the rest of the day.

I was in the middle of one such reverie when a coworker named Ronald Hornfulsch approached me in the break room. Previously I'd regarded Ronald with as much interest as I paid the featureless boardroom decor. He was in his fifties, and his eyes were always directed toward his feet. Despite his middle-aged bulk, he kept his knees too close together, like a shy child.

He shuffled up to me and shook my hand like we'd scheduled a meeting.

"You're Dustin." he said.

I nodded.

"You lost your wife," he said.

I couldn't tell if it were a question.

"My condolences. I've noticed you haven't taken it well." He held out a small card with an address on 38th and Amin's name on it. "If you run out of options, consider this." Then he shambled silently out of the room.

I turned the card over in my hand. On the opposite side, it read *Recondite Services: Personal Items of Immense Weight and Immeasurable Psychic Magnitude.*

I dismissed the card—it sounded like mystical charlatanism—but stowed it away in an unused slit of my wallet. Regardless of the card's validity, it was enough that Ronald had noticed my distraction. I was in danger of losing my job. Coworkers had begun watching me. I'd become an unknown entity, some wild and restive animal let loose in the office. They were waiting, it seemed, for the explosive and frenzied end. They stopped looking me in the eye.

The analytical part of my brain summoned enough strength to try and weather the storm. As a finance manager, I had the flexibility of numbers. I didn't need people for what I did. Most interpersonal communication I conducted over email. So I fell into a routine. I showed up to work in the mornings, fled in the afternoons. I went for long walks, keeping my daydreams of Holly to myself. After a few hours roaming the city, I returned to the office, quiet now, and worked late. I headed home only to sleep.

About this time I also began receiving more of Rebbeca's letters. One every week or so. All of them with her address in Providence clearly marked on the envelope. I still didn't open them. A part of me knew there was something urgent and heavy about the words inside, but I didn't want any part of it. I didn't have the capacity to bear their weight.

On my afternoon walks, my fantasies about a living Holly developed a seasonal quality. Spring, we kept forgetting umbrellas. We must have purchased a dozen new ones. In summer, we attended concerts, swung our arms, and sought refuge from the heat in random drugstores. We sampled Italian ice. As the weather cooled, we bundled ourselves in jackets—mine a brilliant red, hers a shadowy blue with a collar and a silver snap. In the pockets of these jackets we left one another bits of torn paper with writing hastily scrawled—snippets of affection and sometimes tawdry desire placed there as if by an illicit lover. If only for the purpose of these daydreams, I noted the changing weather. As autumn fell, the trees became ornamented in hues that matched the rich sunlight. The air developed an energizing chill. Which is why I remember it was mid-October when Rebecca called again. Feeling guilty, I answered.

She told me she was in town and would like to meet for lunch. There was something broken in her voice, still rattling with grief—I recognized that sound—and despite my reservations, I agreed.

We met at a deli with good coffee and a few tables on the street. We ate outside in our coats. The sunlight soaked into our dark wools. Rebecca's hair was backlit. She smiled and sipped her cappuccino.

"Thanks," she said. "I know how hard this probably is for you."

"We're in it together," I said. I was ready to reassure her again, that it wasn't her fault, even though a part of me still blamed her. I drank my coffee and watched its black surface turn to a tiny tempest in my shaking hands.

"I loved my sister," she said. "But it wasn't the same. I know what it did to you. I know how hard it was, what you went through."

I figured she was repeating whatever it was she'd said in her letters. I didn't have the heart to tell her I hadn't read them. She seemed content not to ask.

"Maybe you never knew," she said, "but I was there when you were in the hospital. I'm the one who called your parents to tell them I thought something was wrong."

I remembered her voice through the door of my apartment.

"I didn't know that," I said. "That you're the one who called them, I mean." Just the thought of it racked me with a wave of paralysis. All the pain of that first few days came at me again. I set down my cup to keep from dropping it.

She reached across the table and put her cold hand over mine. "What I'm trying to convey," she said, "is that I'm not doing this lightly."

"Doing what?" Just the tone of her voice made me feel cornered. "What are you doing?"

"I'm telling you this because it's important that you know."

"Know what? I don't appreciate this, Rebecca."

She remained silent, searching my eyes. "I love you, Dustin."

I stood up almost involuntarily.

"To be clear," she continued, "I don't mean in a brotherly way. Or in the way of two people sharing a loss. I mean, I love you. I always have." She tried smiling, but failed. She was looking up at me, waiting for me to speak.

My knees quavered, threatened to give out, but I steadied myself. "You," I said. I took a breath. "I can't do this. I don't—"

I turned and almost tripped over my chair, then turned back, threw a twenty on the table, and hustled away. If Rebecca called after me, it was lost in the lament of leaves being pulled from the trees by the wind.

III. *The Cost of Therapy*

After Rebecca's confession, my daydreams evolved without my

consent. Holly's face changed. Her thin and elegant nose turned buttonish. Her eyes went a dark gray. Plumper lips. Dimpled cheeks. Until Rebecca was staring at me like she had at the deli. She opened her mouth, and instead of an "I love you," a dark maw opened up and swallowed everything.

I no longer felt relief during my walks. I grew increasingly erratic, fled the office in the afternoons, only to return in minutes. I finished less of my work. My thoughts flocked in unruly waves from memory to workplace to ill-conceived considerations of a real future with Rebecca, which always carried with it the taste of ash. I tried a therapist, but left her because she prescribed medication. I wanted something more surgical, more exacting. I didn't want to drown the world. I wanted to isolate my memories of Holly so that they could no longer contaminate the other parts of me.

That's when I began to ask around about the business card. It was surprisingly easy to find people who'd dealt with Amin, who unabashedly admitted their belief in what sounded like a step above crystal balls and tarot cards. Ronald directed me to a woman in our customer service department, who gave me the number of a florist in Princeton, who told me about others. They all said the same thing: Amin, the proprietor, will help you. He has a calming smile, they said.

My first visit to Amin, I walked out within three seconds. But I continued to lose my grip on the world, to decline. I worked up the nerve for a second attempt. By then, it had been almost a month since Rebecca confessed to me. It would be another week before her letters resumed. And that first one would be thinner than the rest, perhaps a single sheet of paper inside.

IV. *The Cost of a Show*

After giving Holly's underwear to Amin, my first instinct is to retreat to my apartment. But after walking a block or two, I do as he suggested. I go to a show. I overpay the most honest-looking scalper I can find, and I slide into a matinee of *Wicked*. It's something Holly wanted to see for years. Inside, I have trouble keeping my mind on the production. It all turns into a jumble pinwheeling across the stage in brilliant colors, smoke, swelling lights, and echoes. When it's over, I'm out into the late-afternoon fugue of pedestrian and vehicular traffic. I think of returning to Amin's, telling him I don't want to go through with it. In order to avoid going back, I turn up 8th Avenue and pass Columbus Circle. The vegetation there is void of its once summery hues.

I walk along Broadway until I'm looking in at a boutique store advertising an array of high-end designers. The ivory-colored, headless mannequins are wearing women's things—black cocktail dresses and frilled blouses. I'm drawn in without knowing why. A prim red pencil skirt hugs the hips of one mannequin, and I realize I've been staring too long. A faint memory clouds my thoughts. I've been at this window before, I think, gazing in at these expensive things.

The last time I was here though, the mannequin—I'm almost certain—was wearing a pair of black and pink underwear, horizontally striped. Something about the memory of this underwear strikes me as unsettling, even perverse. Have I been thinking about them for years? My fascination with the mannequin's blank white thighs verges on the fetishistic. My attention to its kneecaps even now borders on the obsessive, the criminal, as if I'm one of those men who gets caught masturbating in public after a mental breakdown.

I shiver, either from the cold or the thought, but I can't help standing here just a bit longer. The bottom line is I cannot, for the life of me, figure out why I should care about a pair of striped underwear, an article of clothing I'm certain I've only ever seen in this window display.

I force myself to leave. The feeling of disquiet dissipates as I continue down Broadway.

A few days after seeing *Wicked*, I return to Amin's. He stands behind the counter facing the door, his denim shirt tucked into a pair of khakis. He looks like a high school biology teacher in a place like Frankfort, Kentucky—an anybody, a no one. Not a mystic.

"You're satisfied," he says.

"Is that a question?"

"You went to Broadway? To see a show?"

"I did. *Wicked.*"

"A good one. One I'd recommend."

"That's why I've come," I say. "Because I remember you directing me to Broadway. I remember our conversation in that regard. But I don't remember what I gave you."

He nods. He picks at the flaking skin over his knuckles as if he's not yet interested enough to give me his full attention.

"I also remember you said there was no forgetting."

"Oh, you haven't forgotten," he says. "Your memory has only been shifted to a less harmful place. The couch, remember, has been re-upholstered, toted to a different part of the room so you no longer recognize it. Very big difference. The memory, however, is still a memory, though altered."

"I don't know if I like that."

"There's only one question to ask yourself: Do you feel better than you did last week?"

"I feel like I've lost my keys," I say. "I'm looking around and around for them. I don't know what the memory is anymore, but I *know* it's been misplaced."

"And in this case," Amin says, "you realize you've made the common mistake—the keys are in your pocket. Have been all along. So my question remains: when you reach for the keys, which once were somewhere else, and now which you find in your possession, do you feel better?"

The heat and scent of the air set off deep and unruly hungers in my stomach. Lately I've been eating less. My mind swims.

"Yes. Actually, I feel . . . lighter."

"Then," he says, smiling, "you haven't come to question the method. You've come for another transaction."

He's right.

"But I don't want to lose her completely," I say. "I don't want to not remember my wife."

"That won't happen," he says. "Only details. Take away the details, the story is still the same, but not the pain. Not the passion or the ache."

"Then I want to do it again."

"I thought so. But first, you have to buy something." He spreads his fingers over the display case. Today it's full of items. Random things that look like they've been pilfered from someone's house by an inept burglar. Among a hundred other objects is a VHS tape of *The Little Rascals*. An opened box of Ziploc bags. A 45 of Elton John and Kiki Dee's "Don't Go Breaking My Heart." Dust and scratches mar its grooves. There's also a burnt match, a brown bottle with a torn label, and two toy cars. One is a yellow cab, the other a drag racer missing its tiny front wheels.

"What's the price?" I say.

"I tell you the price once you've picked the item."

"Sounds convenient."

"You know the play *Lady Windermere's Fan*?"

"More broadway?"

"No. Oscar Wilde. In it the famous line: 'What is a cynic?'" He looks at me as if awaiting the answer, then says, "'A man who knows the price of everything and the value of nothing.'" He extends his hand over the case. "These items have been priced based on their value, but I can't trust you to know the value, so I withhold the price until you've selected."

"We're continuing down an arcane path," I say.

"Arcane is only a word to explain the ignorance of the many. You can select and pay, or you can leave. That's not so arcane, is it?"

"Fine," I say. "Fine." I point to the record. "I'll take that one."

He nods. "This one is seven hundred dollars."

"You've got to be kidding me."

"I'm not."

I think about it, but only briefly. "Do you take credit cards?"

He smiles. It's a calming smile, like they say.

V. *The Cost of Postage*

I begin to feel better. Over the next few months, winter descends in relentless rounds of snow that coat the city in gloppy white layers. The snow turns to a mucky dark stew that swashes into storm drains. Heaps grow gargantuan around lampposts and parked cars. Slick slopes climb the walls of warehouses and tenements. Despite the sharp cold, I traipse up 38th to Amin's every few days. The trek is comforting to me now. My reflection in the caterer's window loses its ghostliness. I look the semblance of a more confident, less troubled, man.

The transactions are always the same. Amin offers me an exotic soup or newly risen bread. I sample it, compliment his expertise, his use of spices and rare ingredients—most I've never heard of. He reveals his cooking tips as if telling me state secrets, leaning in and cupping his hand to the side of his mouth. Amin's love of stage productions seems to have given him a knack for the dramatic.

I fork over an object of Holly's. I can't say what the objects are now; every one of them has successfully sluiced into nonexistence with the melting snow. Then I purchase something of someone else's.

These purchased objects begin to collect about my apartment with a quiet ubiquity that renders them harmless. It happens the same way as with any other types of junk. The things from Amin's become stockpiled across the tops of my dresser, bookshelves, in out-of-the-way places like behind a fruit bowl, or in the basket stacked with magazines beneath the television. I'm not, by any means, allowed to throw them out. Not until they lose what Amin calls 'their transactional value.' It's a communal waning, a way for the whole of Amin's customers to spread their pain amongst themselves and thereby lessen woe's potency.

It's late March when I run into Rebecca. She looks bad. We're on the street somewhere near the Bowery. Amin's methods have made it easier for me to sleep, but as a result I've had more energy. On my afternoon walks, I've begun wandering farther afield from my office. I don't wholly recognize the neighborhood.

"What are you doing in town?" I say.

"I came to see you," she says. "I followed you."

Her face is hollow-cheeked, drained of color. She touches the fingertips of her hands together. I notice she's not wearing any gloves, and I remember how cold her fingers were when she reached across the table at the deli.

"You don't look okay," I say. "Let me get you a coffee or something."

She seems not to hear, doesn't react when I motion for her to follow.

"Did you read the letters?" she says.

"I didn't," I say. "I couldn't."

I feel a deep sense of shame. In the sudden relief I experienced after visiting Amin, I never once looked back. I was afraid to. As I slowly lost my daydreams of Holly, I lost Rebecca as well.

"But . . ." she says. She doesn't finish.

"I don't know what to tell you. I wasn't able to. I'm human."

"I just thought . . ." she says.

She extends her arm as if she's going to touch me. Instead, she steps back and hitches the waist of her skirt with her thumb. She yanks it down enough to reveal her underwear. They're horizontally striped. Pink and black.

A hot knife splits my heart. I can't catch a breath. The air condenses to a consistency like wet clay. My throat is closing. Absolutely every last item, every memory, I've given up to Amin, comes back in a red-hot blaze of anger and hurt and helplessness.

The last thing I see is Rebecca, her arms outstretched, trying to catch me as I fall.

I awake in my apartment. When I stand, I have to steady myself against the wall. In the hallway, the closet door is open. The rest of Holly's things, the possessions I was slowly siphoning off to Amin's shop, are gone. The only thing left is a stack of blue envelopes, still sealed, pristine as the day I received each of them and tucked them into the shoebox beneath my bed.

I open them one by one and read what Rebecca wrote to me.

The letters are not letters at all. They're inventories.

At the bottom of each one, Rebecca, in her rigid little script, has written the same thing: I thought of you. This sentence is preceded by a list, sometimes long, other times short. Moments from Rebecca's life. Always followed by that same sentence: *I thought of you.*

Some are simple. *I sat in the sun at the airport. I thought of you.*

Others verge on the effusive. *Leaving work, I spotted an old man in the hospital parking lot. He'd apparently stumbled on the curb and was clutching his knee. I don't know how long he'd been there, but he was just looking up at the hospital, like he might spot somebody in one of the windows and signal for help. I walked over to him, and he noticed my scrubs. He smiled. I smiled back and asked if he needed my assistance. He said no. He said he'd get up when the pain wore off. It was a nice day. He said he hadn't taken time to love a nice day for a long time. He said he was thankful for a little pain if it made him appreciate a day like that. I made sure he was okay, then I left him there. I thought of you.*

They go on this way, a list of sometimes intimate, sometimes bland, instances in Rebecca's life since Holly died. In her own backward way she was sharing. She'd been trying to draw me into her life. Meanwhile, I was trying to remove Holly from mine.

Neither of our plans worked. The pain is throbbing through me now, and I'm in danger of losing consciousness again. I rally in a fit of rage and make my way across town to Amin's. I clutch one of Rebecca's letters the whole way.

In the warmth of the familiar store, Amin stands with his hands on the counter as if he's been expecting me.

"What the hell is this?" I say. I shake the letter and slam it down on the counter.

"You're the one who brought it in," he says. "You tell me."

I pull Rebecca's letter from its envelope. It's the thin one—a single page. It's dated the same day I first entered Amin's shop. I read Rebecca's words. "*Today I purchased a pair of my sister's underwear. Used. Disgusting, I know. Twisted maybe. But I don't know what else to do. I don't know how to make you notice me or how to get you to accept that she's gone. I'm sorry, but after that day when I told you about how I felt, I began to follow you. I found the shop. Amin helped me. I thought of you.*"

Amin stares at me, his face expressionless. No benevolent smile, no solicitous nod.

"How could you do this to me?" I say.

"Do you want your money back?" he says.

"No, I—" I retreat a step. "Everything's back. All my memories of Holly are back."

Amin shrugs.

"What am I going to do?" I say. "God, what am I going to do? I was getting better."

"I apologize for any inconvenience," Amin says.

"You apologize? Did you know?"

"Who she was?" he says. "Oh, yes. She told me who she was."

"You betrayed my trust," I say. I'm shaking I'm so angry. "Why?"

"You keep asking that," he says. He seems to think it over. "The economy," he finally says. He shrugs again. "Times are tough." He gestures toward the room, and for the first time I notice its emptiness. All the cooking implements, the crockpots and burners, are gone. The smell of stew and spices still lingers in the air, but it's already grown stale.

"I have overhead," Amin says. "What can I say? The business of grief isn't self-sustaining." He holds up a finger. "But the business of hope—now there's a venture with value."

"Rebecca was hoping I'd notice her," I say.

Amin nods. "Desperately. So much so she was willing to purchase her sister's undergarments. And for a great deal of money."

"A high value," I say.

"Yes," he says. "A sexual memory, but one tied up with all the intimacy that two people who love one another share over the course of their years together."

"A pair of old underwear," I say. "Valuable." Something in the back of my mind is cracking. I begin to chuckle. It's absurd. Amin has taken us for a ride. Now he's moving out, probably starting a website. Wretched, irredeemable, downhearted fools like me will FedEx him their most precious things from all around the world.

Amin smiles, but this time it isn't comforting. "Buying used underwear to get someone to love you. That's the act of someone lost," he says. "Hoping beyond hope."

"Beyond hope," I repeat. "For a guy who deals in desperation, is there really such a thing as beyond hope?"

"Certainly," he says. "Unless you find someone willing to share the bad with you, along with the good."

It strikes me then that Amin is nothing but a middleman, an intermediary for human connections via whatever knickknacks he trades. I fold Rebecca's letter gently and slide it into the pocket of my coat.

I leave Amin and step out into the old sunlight of the city, the spent gray sky swirling in its volatile way. It's that rainy mood of spring that threatens storms, but might just as easily break and blur into something untouched, something blue and dazzling.

Broken Rebecca, I think. Perfect, broken Rebecca.

I'm wondering what to do next, where to go, when I see her across the street. She's standing, thin and sad with her hands in her pockets.

She's smiling.

ESCAPE

LATE AUGUST HEAT DANCED OFF THE ASPHALT, MAKING RIPPLED visions of the apartment complex. As Joel lifted his lunch pail from the truck, the narrow windows overlooking Bond Street transfigured into glowing absences, hanging there, holding what was left of the day in the lamplight behind the shades. The city sighed. Voices of neighborhood children fluttered by with the leaves.

Before climbing the stairs to Rebecca, Joel tossed up a little prayer, a thanks for Felix Sweeney, a twenty-two-year-old smartass with a penchant for Mountain Dew. He'd caught Felix smoking a joint behind the woodchipper in May and given the kid a second chance. As a result, a month later, when Joel nabbed the position of city maintenance manager, Felix became his staunchest defender against the grumblers and the gripers, the men with seniority who'd been overlooked. Felix held sway over the other men. Something to do with his youth and charisma. He was brash and funny. During lunch, he rattled off tales so perverse the men soaked it up like holy gospel, tears of laughter rolling down their cheeks. Whenever one of the crew groused about Joel, Felix summoned his considerable gift of gab. The kid could shame any man, verbally burn him to ash, and have his comrades howling in the process. So it was Felix—Felix and his campaign of goodwill—that brought the others into line. Because of Felix, Joel felt at peace. He watched the sun tripping into the space behind the park. He let the stars grow. The night came on.

This was how he must have looked—peaceful—as the gunman stepped from behind a delivery van and placed the revolver against his head. His expression must have changed only slightly as the gunman pulled the trigger.

Frank Zsiga pushed back from his desk, which overlooked the bay. The ocean outside the window had gone white about the edges where the water met the gray rocks and folded itself into a frozen foam. In the fireplace, flames made smoke and chirruping pops of the cordwood. Frank threw on another log, then dialed the number for his agent. She answered on the third ring.

"It's episode ten," he said. "It's too mean-spirited."

"Since when are you a prima donna, Frank?"

"The guy who gets shot in the head. What if I care about him?"

"You're supposed to care about him, Frank. The show is set up that way. Build a connection with the audience—a family man, hard-working. Then kill him off so the cop's vengeance makes sense. It's tragedy, Frank."

"But *do* you care?" Rebecca said. She opened the cabinet beneath the sink and jammed the few pages Joel had written into their kitchen trash.

Joel hadn't intended his wife to see the story. Not yet. It had only been a month since what Rebecca referred to as "the miracle." Joel had been standing outside his apartment after a long day's work, and a gunman had stepped up behind him with apparently no other motive than to murder him. Joel had felt the snub-nosed pistol touch the back of his skull. He'd heard the metal clunk of the hammer releasing. That was all. The gunman had cursed under his breath. Frank had turned and seen the man trying to manually rotate the revolver's cylinder. Everything, the whole world, went green and blurry. A swimmy sensation took over. By the time, he consciously told himself to run, the man was already raising the pistol again. This time, though, the man placed the gun against his own temple. This time, the gun fired just fine.

"Do you *really* care?" Rebecca said. "I mean, who the hell cares about a writer? A writer has one flipping job to do: that's think stuff up. And this is what you come up with? A writer? What kind of name is Frank Zsiga anyway?"

Frank Zsiga, he knew, was a flimsy stand-in for God, maybe because Joel couldn't shake his Catholic roots. Maybe because Rebecca's phrase seemed so appropriate. It was a miracle. How else to explain it?

The day he was almost shot, Joel had been driven to the police precinct and given his statement before a detective and a tiny, digital voice recorder. He'd driven over to the city garage the next morning and told the first employee he saw that he was resigning. "Pass the word along," he said.

That employee had been Felix Sweeney.

"The hell you talking about?" Felix said.

"I'm quitting. This isn't what I want to do with my life."

Joel drove home, told Rebecca about his plans to become a writer, and locked himself in their laundry room with a few sheets of printer paper. He didn't own a desk. Not yet. But the the lid of the washer beneath the paper and ballpoint made an intoxicating sound.

The whole thing shook him. Joel comes home—from quitting his job, mind you—and he's like, "I need to write. That's what I always wanted to do. Maybe me almost dying, that's a wakeup call," which is a cliché, right? The near-death experience?

Maybe I'm glossing over the part that, as his wife, makes me look not so hot, not so understanding. After a few hours of him scribbling away, I screamed at him through the door. I called the city and threatened to sue if they went through with his resignation. But in my defense, how ridiculous is that? Wanting to be a writer. It's not like he was an aspiring type. In all the years I've known him, he had no little notepad by the bed. No Saturday afternoons cobbling together a crappy, little novel like every other human being on the planet. I mean, I have that. I have a few ideas. A few characters. But him? Not a single thing.

So here we are, four jobless weeks after the "miracle," and Joel's stuck to his guns. He has this awful story about a guy with a near-death experience, and the story suddenly cuts to a writer. How insane, right? Like I said, how cliché? So maybe that explains me reacting the way I did. Maybe I shouldn't have thrown his work in the garbage—I'll grant you that—but what do you do with that? It wasn't even like the opening was written like a script. The opening—you find out it's from a script, right?—his agent says "episode ten" or something, so the writer is supposedly writing a television show. Tell me then, what's all the prose? Why isn't it formatted like a script?

Dr. Shannon Berk checked the battery on the digital recorder that rested between herself and Rebecca Sala.

"That first part," Dr. Berk said. "About your husband, the backstory about the event and your reaction to his writing. That's *your* writing. You just read it to me straight off the page. So how's that any different from what your husband is doing? How is his writing different than your writing?"

Rebecca clutched her few pages and pulled them close to her body. "I'm in a loop here," she said. "I'm stuck. You start writing about writing, you can't get away from the writing. I'm just doing the therapy to try and work through stuff with Joel." She cocked her head and laughed. "God, there's another cliché, am I right? Exposition through therapy. You're not even a character, Doc. You're a vehicle."

Dr. Shannon Berk didn't laugh. She hadn't become a psychiatrist to be a "vehicle." Perhaps more to the point, she was offended from a writerly perspective. She wouldn't admit it to Rebecca Sala, but her own novel-in-progress—a thriller about a psychiatrist who gets mixed up with the wrong patient, and subsequently pulled into an affair and an unsolved murder—was sitting silently in a folder on the desktop of the computer behind her. She certainly didn't think of her protagonist—the take-no-prisoners Jessica Quinn, with her successful practice in Manhattan—as a vehicle.

Frank Zsiga stared out over the bay toward a distant point. The horizon at dusk turned a sublime gray, and he stood at the window trying to find the line where the ocean lost itself to the sky. He didn't know which one of them was the more powerful, the sky or the sea, only that a demarcation existed. He knew that along that demarcation was the surface of destinies. Men in ships, riding the wind and waves, had changed the face of history. If he could stare long enough, he might be able to see everything, the future, the past, all the ways a story could go.

Ultimately, he retreated to his desk. Work was work. Navel-gazing, even the long-distance kind, was only so useful. What he needed was a regrouping. He wrote, I'm jinxing this a little, maybe thinking it out too much, but here goes:

- *Is Felix Sweeney a part of this story??? why spend time on him if not?*
- *Who was the dude with the gun? why kill himself or try to kill joel MAYBE A FLASHBACK NEXT — WHAT LED TO THE SHOOTING?*
- *Does Joel succeed at .... whatever .... Rebecca and Jo-el's marriage – will it survive????.......Rebecca (too corny a name?)*
- *Come back to me, or does the reader care? too DEM?*
- *Aliens??*

Klatarnoyanaleu, or Klat, weighed five hundred and twenty-eight earth pounds. He stood only five-foot-two in his thickest shoes. Observing humans for the past thirty years had made him self-conscious about his own species' abundance of flesh. The rise in obesity in the United States had helped him blend in some, but he himself wasn't immune to the siren song of high-fructose corn syrup or Jack-in-the-Box. He still got stares when he walked among them.

Yet despite their judgmental nature, he couldn't help but think of humans as creatures in need of compassion. Humans famous, even legendary, in the Tuwiq galaxy for their astounding disregard for historical proofs. Their decisions were almost always instantaneous and impetuous, born of loneliness and heartache. It came down to that, and perhaps it was why Klat forgave them their stares. They were all suffering. They were desperate. So he loved them.

Felix had begun writing *The Epic of Klat*, a space-fantasy opera in four parts. An alien was the protagonist, based primarily on his Aunt Kathy—Kat to her friends—who'd been confined to a motorized wheelchair with diabetes since she was sixty. Felix thought he might give her wings, so to speak. If he could empower Aunt Kat, as an alien, as the upright and compassionate Klatarnoyanaleu, then he could send her on adventures she'd never dreamed of. He could immortalize her, even if he couldn't afford to send her to Florida to see his mother, her own sister, which was the only thing she ever talked about wanting for herself.

But he'd made Klat male, which already felt like a disservice to his aunt. He saved the only two paragraphs of his story on a USB drive before tucking it under his mattress so no one would know about the project until it was a bestselling book.

He emerged from the bedroom.

In the kitchen were Kat and Marcus, a cousin close to Felix's age, who because of a brain trauma when he was seven, was under Aunt Kat's supervision. Aunt Kat and Marcus were shelling peanuts from a giant pile in the center of the table. A little television sitting on a bar stool was playing a rerun of *The Phil Donahue Show*.

His aunt raised her fleshy arm. "Before you ask," she said, displaying a peanut, "they're cheaper in the shell. We're just doing the prep work."

Marcus placed some peanuts into a serving bowl, which was already a third full.

"I didn't say anything," Felix said.

He plunked down, staring at Donahue. What a strange person to have been on television.

"What's on your mind, sweetie?"

"Nothing." He watched a woman on Donahue give a testimonial about finding true love on a camping trip. He cracked peanuts and added to Marcus's pile. Marcus smiled broadly. It was good to see him calm. He'd been making the round of institutions more than usual lately. His meds seemed hellbent on counteracting one another. In addition to his handicaps, he'd been diagnosed last year with schizophrenia. Aunt Kat had cried for days. Felix had found a letter she'd begun to God. It said, "Help us, Lord. I don't know what you're doing up there, but help us to care for each other."

The last few words had petered out. They were lighter and less upright, like she'd lost her nerve. Where she was going to send the letter, Felix didn't know. Maybe she'd intended to burn it and let the smoke roll up to heaven. Felix imagined the smoke drifting into space.

Aunt Kat put her hand on Felix's. "Something's bothering you, I can tell. I got real good senses."

"I think I screwed up."

"Tell Aunt Kat," she said.

"I took a break at work a couple weeks ago." He looked into her eyes and raised his eyebrows, conveying what he meant by "break."

Aunt Kat put a hand to her chest. "Felix Sweeney, you didn't. Please tell me you didn't."

"A quick one. A puff. I was saving the rest for later."

"Who was it? Who caught you?"

"My boss. Or, he just became my boss." He lowered his head. He couldn't take her big, teary eyes.

"And before you go there," he said. "I obviously still got my job."

"How?" she said. "How?"

"He's cool like that, I guess."

"Felix Sweeney, so help me, you ever again—"

"I won't," he said.

"And that's what's bothering you? You needing to get that off your chest?"

"It bothers me," he said, "now he's my boss, he's got that over me."

"I don't understand."

"I get real nervous now thinking if I do the slightest thing wrong, he's going to call me in one day and just go, You're fired."

"That's silly," Kat said. "If he hasn't fired you yet—"

"It's not silly. It's just in the back of my mind is all. You asked. I been wishing he was dead. How messed up is that? I'm thinking, can't something happen to him? Can't he just keel over from a heart attack? Somebody shoot him or something?"

"You don't wish that on anybody," Aunt Kat said. "You stop

talking crazy and cruel and you get your head right. That man saved your job, and this is how you think? With resentment and hate?" She let go his hand and began shelling peanuts again.

She was right, he thought. He had Joel to thank for what tiny amount there was in his bank account. He had Joel to thank for sunny days working slow and getting paid when the boys with the asphalt truck took two hours getting out to the backroads. She was right, and Klat would be right too. That's how you should think of people, with all kinds of love and forgiveness.

Klat would have liked his boss Joel, he thought.

Months go by after the peanut bowl and Marcus can't bear nothing but thinking about Felix sad looking sad and Felix sad and Felix wishing that man dead and the gun and the shoebox and the closet and the going and the going and finally after thinking about it real hard for months now the walking and the drivers moving double fast past Marcus and shouting and saying bad words and the baking heat and then the waiting for the man by his home because Felix pointed it out one time and the man and again and in the truck and then out of the truck and then standing before the truck and a gun and a gun and a gun and a gun and his head and the crummy gun and the clunk and the pushing hard hard hard on the bullets and freeing the gun and knowing oh no knowing you shouldn't kill people and they put you in jail for trying because Donahue talked to a prisoner who said you don't try you don't think and so it's no good and Marcus starts to cry and think of Mama Kat and you don't know because now you can't go back so might as well put the gun to my head might as well me Marcus me don't know now and with nothing in them damn brains but some fuzzy wool and bits of yarn and that's what my daddy said before he left and now it'll be wool on the ground on the street where Felix works on the street with the wool in my head and

The writing had come full circle. According to the laws of whatever narrative existed, Joel should now return to work. The managerial position given to someone else, he'd relinquish his writerly aspirations and take up again with the road crew. He liked the banter anyway, the forklift operator lowering a culvert into a creekbed. He even liked the winter days, the scalding cold when the crew was called to remove a tree that had been waylaid by the weight of ice.

Yes, Joel would give up writing and return. He and Felix one morning would climb into the truck together and Felix would confess, tell him about planting that seed there, in Marcus's head, so full of schizophrenic dryer lint (his phrase). All it had taken was a matchstrike to blaze it out.

"I said I wished you were dead," Felix says to Joel, "and Marcus took me serious."

Felix hating himself the rest of his life. But he would also hang on. As her last act on earth, his Aunt Kat would pay for him to see a psychiatrist, a Dr. Berk, who'd provide him with the 'coping tools' needed. Then Aunt Kat would pass away, maybe from a broken heart. But because Felix had held on, he'd be there for Joel when Rebecca left. He'd visit Joel each night as the other man refused to eat. He'd visit in the morning when he had to dress Joel for work just to get him out the door. That'd be a comfort to Felix—a little— that he could be of help to Joel and to the waning of sorrow on this planet. After all, wasn't that the only thing anyone could do?

Frank Zsiga would one day strip naked and walk into the ocean, his limp body sucked away on the riptide and never returned to shore. The last draft of his half-finished script would remain on his desk, written out like prose and torn apart by his own love for a character he'd been ordered to kill.

Klat, writing his field notes on the human experience could not bring himself to call Frank Zsiga's endless swim a suicide. His compassion for the humans made the bearing of death already too great. One suicide was already too much for one story.

Like any young writer seeking to obtain heights and understanding yet beyond his means, Klat had drawn on the work of his betters, on Faulkner and Chopin, on perhaps Vonnegut, on Barthelme and King. He'd even dabbled in what he considered a postmodern mainstay, fracturing his narrative and attempting to leave meaning out of it. Then he'd relented and tried to put all the meaning back in, feeling wholly unsatisfied by the way the words failed him, even though that's what he knew they'd do.

To be frank, it was the loving that made it all so frustrating. He loved the humans so very much. He felt their pain every second of every day. Recording that pain did nothing but exacerbate his distress at their willingness to let go, to love one another a little and then . . . just let go. In all sorts of ways they forgot themselves, forgot each other, and forgot their own wonder at the late summer heat rising into the twilight.

Klat never could have seen that coming, how quickly the humans forgot, despite all the warnings to the contrary. Maybe that's why they tried writing it down—to remember. But how could you make them understand? He loved them all. He wanted them all, every one of them, to know that his love, or anyone's love, should be enough never to have to write, never to take steps that parsed out the loving and made words of it.

Klat considered this. The field notes had yet to be filed with high command. He set them aside, staring at them as they lay on the glowing helm of his starship. He'd printed and stapled them the way humans liked to do and found the tactile nature of it appealing.

What would the Tuwiq think of this little human tragedy? He didn't know. What would they think of his narrative? It was ham-handed, he knew, a perpetually inadequate document to say what it was to be alive on Earth and also to give that up. His heart ached, as it always did when he came back to these notes. It indeed, as Rebecca Sala had said, looked like cliché after cliché.

He pushed the notes farther from him. He needed a break. In a large compartment containing Earth samples, he'd shelved a great many books. He plucked one out, hoping for a little escapism, a little respite from all the sadness. He opened a bag of peanuts, leaned back, peeled off the book's dust jacket, and cracked the spine.

The opening lines said this:

> *Staring out over the Manhattan skyline was a man with salt-and-pepper hair. He wore an expensive suit that looked like it*

had been slept in. The man was tall and square-jawed, his eyes red with exhaustion.

Jessica Quinn looked into those eyes and had the fleeting thought she might be able to fall in love again. She opened a notepad and readied her pen.

"Now, Mr. Harley," she said, "why don't you tell me how I can help you."

LEADS

BREL IS DIGGING AGAIN. THROUGH THE SMALL KITCHEN WINDOW I see him in the field leaning into the mattock, throwing it over his shoulder and stabbing the earth, the sunset turning his shape into a spindly silhouette. Billie Holiday is on the gramophone and I've fried up flank for dinner, but Brel is digging.

I traipse on out there. The dark earth, the pitted field, hold the heat close while the cool dark sky tries to pry it away.

"You come in now," I say.

"Can't. Got another lead."

Brel is a good man. Came home two weeks ago from the recruiting station and said he'd been deemed unfit for duty. Had a form from the government said tuberculosis had done something to his lungs as a child. Two days later Hominy Archer and her husband, Fred, were about. I walked in from preparing tea to hear Brel telling them he was on a special assignment from the government. That's why he was sticking around.

Fred leaned forward in his chair. "You telling me you're working for the army? But they want you to just keep breaking clods on that old Iowa field?"

"That ain't exactly right," Brel said. "Just can't talk too much about what they do want me doing."

Fred nodded, skeptical, and Hominy, for want of other conversation, complimented the look of my apple fritters.

Next day Brel was in the field digging. First time in ten years we hadn't risen together. Half a cup of cold coffee sat near the sink with a bit of gristle from the spring lamb I'd prepared the night before.

That morning I just watched from the window. I fixed lunch, and he came in to eat it. He'd dug half a dozen holes and half a crop of kale up with it.

"Why are you tearing up what we just put in the ground?" I said.

He looked up from his mashed potaters and set down his fork.

"I'm working for the United States Army. That's all I'll say."

"You said the United States Army gave you the brush off. Since when did they give you some orders you ain't told me about?"

"Since they told me not tell you," he said.

Next day he was at it again. Four in the morning I heard the bed springs sigh, felt his hands at my back as he tucked the blanket against my body to hold in the warmth he'd left me like a keepsake.

Two in the afternoon he came to the porch with a grin. His chin had stubbled, and sweat stains had attracted dirt into muddy patches about his armpits and neck. In his hands he held a wooden box with a padlock, which he pried off with a jimmy bar. Inside were a set of papers all typed up and folded, neat as a lawyer's file.

"You know what this means?" he said.

"No, I don't," said I. "And I'm about ready you tell me."

"Means I got more digging to do."

Couple months back Brel and I lost our son to the war in Europe. Caught pneumonia and died in France. Few days after that all Brel talked about was quitting farming, selling the place, setting me up near Sioux City so he could join the army, and go and fight. He's still young enough, he tells me. But after what they told him at the recruiting station, he's gone sort of silent like. At night he says he might try the station in Ankeny, where he's heard they're more lenient. But he's resigned himself to the digging, I can tell. You can't take vengeance on the frost, anyway, I tell him. Or the cold, which is what killed our boy. We buried our boy's quilt near the oak tree out back to mark the spot where we'll lay his body when he's shipped back to us. I keep watch on it from our sitting room window. Practice I suppose for the day I can look out on my son resting in the ground.

Nine days after he starts, Brel is still digging.

On our porch are five boxes with broken padlocks, each with typed letters I've never read.

The holes make a wide circle around the oak and our son's grave-to-be.

"Got another lead," he says, turning and turning the earth.

I want to give him a good look at my fists. His beard has come in. It's gray in spots, which I didn't know about on account he's always been clean-shaven. His clothes need washing. I crept downstairs a week ago and scrubbed them, then threw them out on the line to dry. When he arose before dawn you'd have thought he was being stabbed the way he hollered putting on wet duds. He didn't talk to me that day, but he found two boxes. The last one he dragged into our bedroom after midnight and read the letter by lamplight.

I rolled over in the bed and asked him then if I could read what was written, and he told me if he caught me looking at army secrets he'd march me up to the sheriff's station and have me arrested on grounds of national security.

Three weeks later, we're still in the field, and Brel is digging same as ever. He looks a wreck.

"This is some prank them boys in the office is playing on you," I say. "Can't you see that?"

"It's army secrets," he says. "And I got to follow the leads."

He coughs into a handkerchief. There's blood in his nose. Cold vittles in the morning is all he's eaten since I questioned him that first day at lunch. His face has withered down to sheared bone.

I turn and leave him with his leads. I've had enough.

On the porch I fling open all thirteen boxes and gather the papers. They're crisp in my hands. I recognize the broken Q and the blunted R of the old Royal typewriter we keep in the attic.

I read them all.

After I've sat a while, I start to reckon the questions here are better suited to the wind than the ground. I throw the pages toward the sky. They sail like doves caught in a storm.

If Brel asks where they went, I'll tell him it was the army. They came and took the letters. By God, they came and took it all away.

FIERCEST TRAITS

BEYOND THE RIDGE THE ROAD TOOK A TENDER TURN, CLIMBING free of the trees and tearing itself from the ivy that walled in either side of the road. Tom could imagine it, a mere forty seconds away. The sudden relief of topping the hill, the vegetation thinning until the land spread out before him. Up there the road scampered along a spine of freedom.

"It's just a perfect view," he told Mary. "You won't believe it."

Mary shrugged. She was seven and in the habit of disregarding his newest round of 'bridge-builders,' activities the Christian counselor at the Baptist church told him would help recover the ground lost in the divorce. He'd slapped together a decent list of things he and Mary could do that would, as the counselor put it, 'cross the gap between your loves and hers.' Couldn't be pandering, he was told. Couldn't tote her off to a rollercoaster park or an ice cream shop. That wasn't what this was about. It was about creating common ground. So far, fireworks at the gun show, fishing, canoeing, and rappelling had all met with her stonewalling gaze, her unimpressed sighs, and a general apathy as formless and insurmountable as one of these old mountains cloaked in stormclouds.

As if mocking him, the stuffed alligator that he'd purchased yesterday, with its bead-brown eyes and felt teeth, sat between them on its back, untouched, as if it had died there of neglect, its tag still stabbed through its left foreclaw, its bright red tongue lolling to one side.

The truck reached the ridge and instead of the burnt gold frock of last sunlight torching the valley with heavenfire, there was nothing but the still grayness of an overcast and lackluster evening, the humdrum shift-change from day to night. There was no fanfare. No precious view of God's ample blessings. Tom's heart bottomed out.

Well, shit, he thought.

He pulled the truck to the side of the road where he sometimes sat for hours just contemplating the dark green slope of these Appalachian hills. Tonight they looked not only plain but small. He was certain, Mary living in Cincinnati now, the stadiums and concert halls, the glistening office-buildings, all had more grandeur than this, his humble little piece of West Virginia.

"It's normally better than this," he said weakly. Mary hadn't hugged him in seven months. He thought it was early yet for when girls got all squirrelly about their bodies. He was thankful for that, of course, because he wouldn't have known what to do with an adolescent female even if she came with a manual. Still, it bothered him that his little girl had, seemingly without provocation, put up an invisible barricade.

She stared down the mountain in the direction he'd hoped she would, and for a second he thought, despite everything, she was still managing to see the beauty here, the reason why he'd stayed when Alyssa gave him a chance to come with her. Alyssa had called him chickenshit when he refused to move. They'd been through rough seas before, but whatever anchor kept him bound to this place had sunk the marriage completely.

Theirs was a tale not unlike those of a lot of doomed couples, their particular riff on the old saw being the one in which a career, hers, takes on the proportions of a third member in the relationship. As this happened, they fought constantly.

They're using you, he'd told Alyssa. By then she'd made a name for herself as a sculptor. *Aesthetica* and *ArtNews* called her stonecarvings the foremost force in the twenty-first-century craft revival, elevating the form to the minimalism of Sol Lewitt and Robert Graham. Tom knew what it really meant, though. She was a country girl from the sticks with a little bit of talent. They wanted her because she was a discovery. She was a thing they could pull out of the ground and tote around and put on display so they could say, look here, look what we did. It was easy enough to strike talent in SoHo or Paris or wherever it was you spotted artists, but it showed panache to find this skinny-armed chick with a nose ring and calloused fingers in a backwater with a cinderblock building full of sandstone deathmasks, shale impressions of rivers, and limestone busts of forlorn figures she created from woodcuts depicting the black plague of the fourteenth century. Now that was a find. That showed their insight, their sensitivity to true talent. It validated them. That was all.

Then she'd been offered a job, a real job, in the art department at UC. The last night they spoke in person, he told her she'd be back as soon as she wasn't a novelty. That was four years ago, and she continued to climb. She sent him an article from *The New York Times* where she was interviewed. On the back, she wrote, *Still going, asshole*. Now every two months he got Mary. Mary clomped down the oversized steps of a Greyhound and he picked her up at the tackle shop near Otis's Carryout. He thought about some man in *The New York Times* office asking his ex-wife questions over the phone.

How do you build a bridge from here to New York? the man had said. He'd been referring to the vast, cultural difference between Alyssa's childhood in a trailer park behind a Dollar General and her next show, scheduled to open at the Opera Gallery at the beginning of the year.

Bridge-building, Tom had thought ruefully.

Now his thoughts returned to Mary beside him in the truck. She nibbled on her thumbnail. "We done yet?"

"I'm not kidding. The view is normally prettier." He started the truck back up.

The next day Mary claimed to have a "ticklish throat," a phrase he was certain she picked up from one of Alyssa's cohorts at the college or from one of those skinny, pale creatures, always men, who occasionally appeared with her in photographs.

He demanded to feel Mary's head. "If it's a fever, I need to know about it."

"I'll scream if you touch me," she said fiercely.

"So, no activities today?"

"I need to rest."

He left her alone in front of the television in his stale-smelling living room. The rest of the day she commented aloud at the lack of channels and the poor quality of the picture on his outdated television set. He cooked her grilled cheese and tomato soup, and she picked at it as if it were some suspect dish in a third-world country.

As night covered the windows, he stood in the kitchen, staring through the doorway. She was still in her pajamas, still wrapped in a blanket, and occasionally rubbed her throat for dramatic effect. When his phone rang, she didn't look over. On the other end of the line, James Cooper spoke so fast Tom had to slow him down four times before he could make out the words being said. "They got one of them personal zoos out on Jisco West Road. Some guy with about a thousand monkeys and lions let 'em all loose, then shot himself in the head, the dumb asshole."

"What's that got to do with us?"

"All hands on deck," James said. "They got local sheriff's office up there." He paused for effect. "Also a bunch of guys from the volunteer fire department."

"Us?" Tom said.

"Damn straight. I'm headed out. You'll see it. Look for the lights." He hung up.

There was a moment, the phone still in his hand, staring at his daughter's little, sharp nose, her proud lips in profile, that Tom hovered between two ideas. The first involved him continuing to mope about the kitchen while Mary rested like a perfect statue on his couch. He disregarded it almost immediately and went with his second idea: striding into the living room, he blocked the screen.

"That was a friend of mine from the fire department."

She glanced at him, betraying her interest.

"It's not a fire," he said. "What he called about, my friend from the fire department—it wasn't about a fire."

She lolled to one side, watching the left side of a Cialis commercial.

"What he called about—it's a zoo. A bunch of animals got out."

Her gaze lifted slowly. She switched from biting her thumbnail to her index finger. He recognized this as Alyssa's tell, when she was interested.

"Who let them out?" she said softly.

"Ah, never mind. It's an emergency, and they need my help, but I couldn't take you. That'd never work. I don't even know what I was thinking."

Her eyes focused on him as if just now adjusting to the plane of reality in which he existed. Her round face and sharp chin, the thick auburn hair and small nose, were all Alyssa's, and it was like when Alyssa used to ask him for favors. Even in the final throes of their marriage, she'd smile slyly, her head tilted downward so her eyes met his from a lower, more beggarly angle.

"Can we go?" Mary said.

"Absolutely not. Your mother would do terrible things to me if she knew." He was testing her.

"I wouldn't tell. Never," she said.

"No. It's out of the question. Too dangerous."

She leaned forward and put her small hand on his forearm. Ripples of electricity rolled up his elbow into his shoulder. This was also something Alyssa used to do, too. She used to make sure he was listening by making contact, bridging the gap to get his full attention.

"Dad," Mary said. "Can we go? I really want to see the animals."

Jisco West Road s-curved up a lazy slope, then dropped off dramatically into a valley. Heavy rains in spring always washed half the hillside down. More than once Tom had helped the city maintenance crew remove downed trees, always four or five guys with chainsaws and pickup trucks tossing that winter's firewood into their beds. At the bottom of the hill, near a creek was a mud-and-gravel drive held together by pine needles. It led back to a rusty double-wide where an old guy named Yerian kept animals. Mostly llama, Tom had heard. He'd also heard the guy fought cocks, and he'd seen the distinct blue barrels on their sides, the ends cut out, each with a Kelso rooster strutting about on a chain like a leashed dog.

He parked the truck near the road.

"Don't you dare move," he told Mary.

"I want to come," she said.

"No, sir. There are men with guns out there. And wild animals."

"That's why I want to come." She had Alyssa's knack for undeniable logic.

"If we catch one, I'll let you see it. We'll get the animals back in their cages. Then you can see. But right now, it's not a place for little girls."

"I'm not little. I've been to the Guggenheim. Have you ever been to the Guggenheim?"

"That doesn't have anything to do with it."

"I've been to the Taipei 101," she said.

"I don't know what that is."

She studied her fingernails as if considering a manicure might be in order. "It's in Taiwan. You've probably never been to Taiwan, either."

This was news. "When did you go to Taiwan?"

She shrugged her impossibly small shoulders. "Mommy went there because a man liked her robot."

He had a little context, but only a little. Alyssa's newest series re-imagined the *maschinenmensch*, the female automaton from Fritz Lang's *Metropolis*, as an ancient deity. The carvings were stylized idols made to resemble the heads of Easter Island using the face of Maria, the movie's heroine on whom the robot was based. As Alyssa's career took off, her work had become more political. The heads were five feet tall. They supposedly commemorated lesbians hunted by the Nazis. That seemed to be the consensus, anyway.

"It's also a way of taking back what Hitler stole from Lang," she'd told *Kunst Magazin*. "I try to reimagine what it might be like—a bold feminine power as the force of long-term revolution, rather than a subjugated entity." At the base of these towering, female robot goddesses were smaller idols broken to bits. The faces of these ruined idols were modeled after Leni Riefenstahl's. Tom didn't know what most of this meant, only that he'd read it dutifully and clipped the articles and ordered the impossibly expensive subscriptions whenever he could get them. Silly as it was, he envisioned some future dialogue with Alyssa in which she copped a superior air, and he countered with his erudition about her career and the art world in general. Thus far, that hadn't happened.

He held his breath and touched Mary's forearm. She didn't pull away. He was encouraged.

"You mean the Fritz Lang sculptures?"

She looked bored. "I don't know," she said. "Just robots."

He let go. He made a mental note to look up "Taipei 101." At the very least, he'd figure out where Taiwan was.

"I'll be right back," he said. "Stay here."

She crossed her arms and looked ahead at the glove box. He lifted his .22 out of the rack in the rear window and locked the doors. Standing at the mouth of the drive, he stared back at Mary, her moon-white face as implacable as one of Alyssa's statues. He trudged up the dark hill through the trees. About fifty yards in he saw the trailer, rust-strewn, bloated with the weight of its own roof. Its flimsy sides were bowed outward. A few windows had been busted and replaced with duct tape and cardboard pizza boxes. Near the trailer was a single cruiser, its spotlamp trained on a section of woods beyond the trailer.

"Ho," Tom shouted. A deputy near the car held up a hand.

"That you, Tom?"

"Sure. What do we got?"

He saw, as he drew closer, the deputy was Zach Taylor, a guy he'd played football with in high school.

"It's a mess back there, Tom. No one's allowed inside the house 'cept the coroner and the sheriff."

"What about the rest?"

"Monkeys mostly, they think. The llamas are still in the pen. They have to shoot the monkeys, though."

"What the hell for?"

"Can't take the chance. You know how strong a monkey is?"

"Big monkey?"

"Chimpanzee, I think."

"That's an ape."

Zach Taylor looked at him like he was still waiting for him to speak.

"How many guys?"

"Just the three. James, Chad, and Ronnie."

"James said it was a bunch of different animals."

"Nah. Everybody thought that because of how it happened a few years ago—that guy up north who did the same thing, only with tigers and cheetahs and stuff." Taylor gestured toward the back of the trailer like an especially congenial butler. "Holler back so you don't get shot."

Tom rounded the trailer and called out. He heard James somewhere in the underbrush hiss to him in a stage whisper. "Hang on, Tom. I'm coming." James appeared out of a thicket of greenbrier, a smile so wide Tom could make out James's crooked teeth in the dark. James handed him an extra flashlight and led him back. The faint cluck and scratching of roosters came from nearby.

"He had a place set up," James said. "Out of view."

Deeper in, obscured from the road, was a row of cages cobbled together out of chainlink and barbwire. A corrugated tin roof, chewed through with rust and rigged over with a blue tarp and patches of old shingling, constituted what must have been scant shelter in the winter months for whatever animals were inside. A mucky, rich stench hit Tom as he neared it.

"Had 'em pinned back here," James said.

"Just monkeys?"

"Apes," James corrected. "Chimps and maybe a gorilla. Can you believe that?"

"How many?"

"Hard to say. A dozen cages or so. But we don't know how many were in each one. Sheriff says to shoot on sight."

"What if they're friendly?"

"Don't matter. They're dangerous."

Tom felt a deep sickness like a black stone in his gut. He couldn't imagine shooting a monkey or an ape. He'd seen too many movies with close-ups of their eyes. The thrill of seeing a tiger or a boa constrictor or, hell, a duck-billed platypus, had seemed like his chance at giving Mary an exotic experience, something she would remember fondly for decades, tell stories about at cocktail parties or at whatever events people went to in Cincinnati. Instead, it dawned on him that what he'd done was something stupid. How much stock could he put in a seven-year-old's vow of silence? If Alyssa found out he'd brought Mary to the woods where grown men were shooting primates, Mary's visits would stop entirely. He'd never see his daughter again.

"I'm going," he said.

James pleaded. "Come on, Tom. We need you. We can't have one of these things get away."

Tom didn't stop. He could hear James mewling over not enough manpower as he went. Halfway down the drive, he saw his truck parked along the road under a splash of moonlight. He felt like a nothing in the trees, a black and shapeless bit of summer air. Mary couldn't see him, but he could see her. She was tapping out something on the dashboard, maybe practicing for piano. She might be doing anything. He didn't know her anymore. She was just a kid, and he didn't know her. Just a kid he sometimes talked to and fed and let run his thermostat when she was in his house.

He was about to take a step when he saw the monkey run into the drive. Backlit from the open space of the road, it was one of those monkeys you always saw dancing for organ grinders in old movies. Maybe a foot tall with a round, fuzzy head and white face. Its eyes seemed to judge him, and Tom shuddered. He still had James's flashlight and flicked it on. Now the monkey's eyes were huge and brown with an eerie, gold iridescence. Mary noticed the light and then the monkey. She was out of the truck before Tom could stop her.

"That's far enough," he said. She edged forward.

"It's dangerous," he said.

"He's so little." She worked her fingers in a come-here gesture.

"Don't do that," he said. But she wouldn't stop. He considered stomping to scare the thing off, but that might send it scurrying her way. Instead, he mimicked his daughter, trying to coax it. He whistled through his teeth. "Here, monkey-monkey." He snapped his fingers. The little thing perked. "Here, little fella." He snapped his fingers again, and the monkey ran for him. His stomach went cold. A monkey was running in his direction—a wild animal whose temperament and ferocity were unknown. He tried to remember if he'd ever heard of an organ grinder's monkey ripping a man's face off. It padded along on its black feet, knuckling the ground in full stride. Its white-fanged mouth was open as if it might scream. Little hoarse noises arose from its throat.

Despite his fear, he kept the gun lowered. He wasn't about to point it in Mary's direction. The monkey leapt, caught hold of his knee. Tom felt its tiny hands grasp his jeans. Then it launched itself up to his chest and onto his shoulder. The chuffing noise was in his ear now, the monkey out of breath. Its miniature fingers clutched a wad of his hair. The monkey's weight was like a sack of flour poised on his shoulder. He could feel the warmth radiating off its fur. He smelled the deep animal scent of it, like the corners of a barn.

"Daddy, you got him," Mary said. A happiness swirled inside her voice.

"Don't come any closer."

She marched forward with her hands on her hips. It was the walk, he thought, of a grown woman who means to chide you for tromping across the carpet in your workboots.

"Daddy, you look stupid. Maybe you'd better let me hold him." She reached for the monkey. He heard the monkey hiss, a half-gargle like a high-pitched growl.

"Better not, babe."

She stomped. "You're just keeping him to yourself."

"He's dangerous."

"You're hogging the monkey."

"I want to keep you from harm. That's all." But something was stirring in his mind, a slow-cooker of an idea. Finally, he said, "You really want to hold him?"

She nodded vehemently, her hair bouncing like a pom-pom.

"Then I need you to promise me something."

"I won't tell, if that's what you mean."

"That's not it. I want you to do something different than that." The monkey's breathing ramped up. He felt it wheezing across his cheek. "I want you to call me from your house."

She looked puzzled. "I already do that."

"I want you to do it without your mom knowing, when she has people over. To the studio. I want you to let me listen."

He could tell he was confusing her, frustrating her desire to pet the animal.

"All you have to do," he said, "is the next time your mom is showing someone around the studio—I know she does that sometimes for people who want to buy her work—I want you to call me and then carry the phone in without your mom seeing. I just want to listen."

She frowned. "You want to spy."

"It's a game," he said. He lowered himself to Mary's height. She eyed the monkey longingly. I'm going to hell, he thought. After prison, straight to hell. But he needed something more, some insight into the life Alyssa was leading now. If he were ever going to have Mary back, he needed Alyssa back, and to do that he had to know the new Alyssa. He had to hear her, to know her new language in her new life.

"That's all I have to do?" Mary said.

"That's all." He hadn't understood how lonely he was, how much he missed Alyssa, until now, not until he leaned forward and let a wild monkey leap into his daughter's arms. He felt its tiny feet bound off his shoulder, saw it nimbly land at Mary's feet.

She knelt down, but he stopped her.

"Don't grab," he said.

She stood stiffly while the monkey clambered. It swung around to her back and placed a furry foot on either of her small shoulders. Its tail whisked across her nose and mouth, and she made a *pppfffffftt* sound. The monkey's hands met in her forehead like a furry crown. Its head rested atop hers. Its eyes and Mary's were both wide and wild with fear and delight. Their excitement and expectation seemed to charge the air with possibilities. A high breeze blew through the trees, sending the leaves to singing. A moment. Then a gunshot. The echo of it rolled out of the hills. Tom spun in the direction of the trailer. Men were shouting now. Their voices were short, shrill barks, like dogs with a scent.

"We have to go," he said. But Mary was looking into the trees beyond the road. She was waving. The monkey was gone. He hustled her to the truck.

On the ride home she didn't speak. It was as if the silent moment with the monkey hovered there, an invisible remnant of something mystical. The silly stuffed alligator he'd purchased for her trip was still on the seat between them, a reminder that tonight had been just one in a number of attempts to gain Mary's favor. But now she smiled, pressing her hand into the alligator to lean toward him.

"I liked that," she said.

There was something different about her face now. She was somewhere far off but also present at the same time. She pressed her cheek against his shoulder for just a moment. Not a hug, but a dam broke loose inside of him and threatened to throw him into full-bodied sobs. He need to have something to focus on to stave off absolute breakdown, in order not to be washed away in his own emotional wellspring, so he watched Mary's hand grinding the little alligator out of shape.

They drove on. The fear drained out of him slowly. His legs felt rubbery as he worked the clutch, the gas, the brake. His small house, its windows still softly shaded in the faint blue of curtains Alyssa had hung, had never looked so safe. His thoughts remained wordless and fuzzy as he unlocked the front door and let Mary in. She climbed the narrow stairs to her old bedroom, and he heard her brushing her teeth with the special electric toothbrush with the sonic head.

He wanted to shout up, to tell her it was still early and he could make her some food. She seemed to like criticizing the paucity and inferiority of his cuisine. At least she'd be talking, and by that he'd be able to guess her mental state, whether she were giddy or traumatized or some girl-version of emotional he couldn't guess at. But he said nothing. Waiting for her at the bottom of the stairs, he wondered why he hadn't asked Mary for a hug—why a hug from his daughter hadn't been the genie's wish he put forth in exchange for her being allowed to hold the monkey.

Seven months, and practically all he thought about when she was with him was a hug, what her small arms would feel like lassoing his neck or half-encircling his chest. A hug would mean something. Yet he hadn't asked for that. Maybe he didn't want her affection to be a bartered thing. But ultimately he decided that it was Alyssa. He loved Mary, of course, but Alyssa was the thread that bound them. Or rather, she was the bridge itself. The newly established distance between Tom and his daughter had made that clear. Alyssa's strength, her incredible capacities, had held them all together, but it hadn't survived the distance.

He sat down on the bottom step and imagined what might happen next: Mary descending, already changed into her pajamas. "Good night, Daddy," she'd say. Still giddy from the night's events. He might get his hug yet. He'd close his arms around her and feel the warmth rolling up off her small back. He'd think of the monkey, the heat he'd felt. He'd wonder what the animal's odds were out in the woods, even if it avoided the men. "Good night, monkey," he'd say to Mary. She wouldn't acknowledge his little joke. She'd let him go, squeeze his hand, pressing her thumb lightly into his palm the way he used to do when she was much younger, his wordless, little *I love you*.

But Mary didn't come back down, didn't hug him or squeeze his hand. An hour later, he went out to the truck and retrieved the alligator, returned with it and mounted the stairs quietly. She'd left the door open to her bedroom. She was still awake, staring up at the ceiling in the darkness. He wanted to tuck the alligator in beside her and see her squeeze it to her side. But he could tell she was thinking of the monkey. She was remembering it, reconstructing a few brief seconds in meticulous detail. He remained silent, retreated to his bedroom, and took the alligator with him. He laid it in the bed beside him and stared at its bulging eyes, its teeth, its tongue, until he fell asleep.

When he drove her to Otis's Carryout two days later, she still hadn't said anything about the monkey. He hadn't either. In the early morning, a debilitating fear had overtaken him again that Mary would tell Alyssa what had happened. The longer they kept it unsaid, the better hidden it felt to him. Before the bus doors, he said, "See you next time."

She looked up at him, stepped forward, hesitated, then shuffled back. He held out the alligator to her, but she pretended not to notice. She hopped onto the bus, her overly serious, black backpack jingling with all her girly trinkets inside.

That night, he did some serious gazing at the ceiling himself. He held on to what he could of his memory of Mary's visit. But something felt irrevocably faded. He couldn't hold on to the memory of her features. Not like Alyssa. Once, when Alyssa was first discovered, the director of a gallery in São Paulo had come to "inspect" her art. He'd run his hand over a soapstone relief that Alyssa had done of a neighbor woman and said somewhat derisively, "You have a simple, little style." He seemed about to leave when Alyssa took his hand and placed his thumb down into a blot of spilled ink. She lifted his thumb and pressed it down onto a scrap of sketch paper like an arresting officer. It left a black print. She then clipped a sheet to her easel and, without ever looking away, began drawing with a stub of pencil. In under thirty seconds she'd sketched a very large, very rough version of what looked like a thumbprint with far fewer whorls. The man, still wiping his hand on a rag, stared down at the blot his thumb had made, then up at Alyssa's drawing. He did this several times, inspecting his print and Alyssa's sketch for nearly ten minutes. He suddenly beamed. He hugged Alyssa, chattering away. Half his words dove into Portuguese. He left still jabbering, his window open, his voice carrying all the way down the road.

Six months later, Alyssa was practicing her *oi*, her *onde é o banheiro?*, her *boa noite*. It wasn't until after she'd left for the show in Brazil that Tom took a good look at her crude drawing. He found it discarded in a corner of her studio, along with the thumbprint of the Brazilian man. It took Tom a very long time, longer than the director, but he saw that Alyssa had replicated the strongest lines, the most prominent features, in the man's thumbprint. She'd seen them that quickly. The center of the whorl, the radiations, the seeming flaws, she'd lifted and highlighted so that all that remained were the distinctions, the fiercest traits. The man had caught her meaning and understood that Alyssa's seemingly rough-hewn style was a depiction of the deepest self, the bare truths of a person's makeup.

Tom had no such capacity. Lying in the dark, his vision of Mary trembled and wavered. It ran like a soppy watercolor. Mary's face blended itself with other children he'd known when he was young. She became indistinct except as a version of Alyssa. My own daughter, he thought. My own daughter. He reverted to staring at the stuffed alligator, as he had on numerous nights since Mary's visits, but realized, as if struck with a mystical revelation, why she'd rejected it. It didn't remind her of anything. The alligator was distinctly inhuman—its long, green snout, its terrible jaws, its flat feet and triangular toes were ferocious and discernible, but provided no bridge between memory and human need. By buying her the alligator, Tom had proven he knew nothing about love. Just before sleep took him he resolved to find Mary a stuffed monkey and present it to her the next time she came.

A week later he got a call. He was in his car on a lunch break outside the cabinet factory where he worked. The stuffed monkey and stuffed alligator sat in the seat beside him. A sandwich in wax paper rested on his thigh. "Hello?" A muffled noise, a door, and music in the distance. He checked the number. Alyssa's. He pressed the phone to his ear. He could hear Alyssa humming along to the radio in the background, the way she used to in her makeshift studio behind their house. He listened like this until his lunch break was over, then hung up. He felt mended and solid. It wasn't until the evening that he thought how proud he was of Mary for thinking of calling him at that time of day, during his lunch break, when she knew he'd be available. So smart, he thought. So very smart.

The calls continued for a couple weeks, intermittently, always during his lunch break. Listening to Alyssa, just the clatter and shuffle of her movements, made him whole. Sometimes he put the phone on speaker, chewing his sandwich as he, the monkey, and the alligator listened to Alyssa work. Then on Wednesday of the third week, he caught something more. Alyssa's voice was strewn between hiccups of sound—two, maybe three, people moving in the room. The words were broken but for a few.

"Sabbatical to Taiwan," Alyssa said. "We've been there once to talk with the head of the foundation."

Another voice. The lilt of a question.

"A year or two, most likely."

He listened longer to snippets of technical articulation, philosophical concerns over the reception of her pieces in foreign countries, none of it as thrilling as he'd once thought it might be. At the end of it, he heard the phone being jostled and Mary's sudden, high voice speaking in a whisper. "I want to see the monkey again," she said. "Before we go." The line clicked dead before he could respond.

That same night, James gave Tom the list of animals the sheriff and a few hunters had killed since their escape. Two young baboons. A squirrel monkey. "A real bust," James said. "There's a gorilla probably out there ready to tear someone to pieces." The division of natural resources had been notified, along with the dogcatcher. Tom didn't mention the organ grinder monkey. He began to wonder if he'd imagined it.

Instead of watching the sunset from his favorite spot that night, he drove down Jisco West Road and sat where he'd parked with Mary. A chain had been strung across the old man's drive and rigged with an aluminum sign. *NO TRESPASSING*. Attached to the chain was still a laminated piece of paper declaring the property a crime scene.

He thought of what his own defining traits might be, of what Alyssa saw in him when they were first married. He guessed it might be his perseverance. He'd recognized that Alyssa was special before anyone else. Even before she herself could define her gifts, he'd followed her blindly from her day-job at Reynolds' pharmacy to her night-job at the Corner Pub, offering her rides in his new Camaro, despite the fact the pharmacy and bar were only three blocks apart. She'd turned him down but was smitten—even a dense old boy like him could see it—by the way he loved her so immediately, and by the way he kept after it. Weeks. Months. Until she finally said yes, like she finally believed in the vision of herself that he saw. Maybe it was the same reason things hadn't worked out. Since he'd followed her everywhere, maybe she had thought that he'd follow her right out of town when the time came. He hadn't, and right now couldn't remember why. It was as if everyone else finally seeing how special she was made his own knowledge of that fact insubstantial, less valuable. He'd stopped following her, and by the time he'd realized his mistake, she was too far gone to make up the distance.

He stepped from the truck and wandered into the woods, snapping his fingers, whistling through his teeth. "Here, monkey-monkey." He tried whispering it. "Monkey," he said. "Monkey-monkey." He crouched down, sniffing the air for that scent. In the distance he could see a sycamore, its ghost-pale bark blotted with brown splotches and standing out against the shadows. The white branches shivered in the scant wind. He steadied himself on the balls of his feet, placing a hand to the ground. He focused, unblinking, settling his gaze on a bough halfway up.

"I see you, monkey," he said. "I'm going to get you."

*

Alyssa called one afternoon the following week. She was steely, ready for whatever fight she thought he was going to put up. He let her talk a while. She laid out all her arguments as to why Mary should come to Taiwan. "We're scheduled to leave in a month," she said. "We'd be there for two years, but we'd fly back occasionally. You could see her then if we had the time." She was letting him know she didn't intend to let Mary return to West Virginia before they left.

"I understand," he said, "about everything. Cultural experience. All good for Mary. I wish you the best." He could hear her tapping the phone with her finger.

"I expected," she said, "you to say something less reasonable."

He imagined a page of notes at her desk with a list of benefits to Mary's future.

"I can be reasonable," he said.

Then it was her turn to surprise him. "We could make a special trip, come down this weekend," she said. "Before we go. I'm not out to hurt you, Tom."

He thought about it, about the two of them coming for a visit. Then he thought about Mary and how she'd asked for only one thing, something he hadn't yet acquired. He glanced at the stuffed monkey sitting on the kitchen table. It and the alligator were with him always now. They were like reminders of what love was and wasn't.

"I don't think I'll have time," he said. "I have a few irons in the fire, a few business things."

Alyssa laughed. "What are you up to these days, Tom? A little day trading? Black market guns? This is exactly that thing, Tom. The thing you do. You get this idea that life has to be a certain way."

"A certain way," he repeated.

"It's why we didn't work. You were set. And now you're not seeing your daughter because you have 'irons in the fire'?"

It'd be good to let them come. But he didn't want Alyssa shoving Mary forward and forcing her to hug him. That's what it came down to. He could envision Mary sheepishly standing, eyes downcast, forced into it, waiting for the contact. It made him feel ill just imagining that scene. Instead, he wanted her to see something in him. He wanted Mary to spot something even Alyssa couldn't see, and by doing so make Alyssa see it too. And if this feat had to be accomplished by his capturing the monkey, then so be it. He'd follow the animal the way he'd followed Alyssa. And this time he wouldn't let it go.

"Just take care of Mary," he said. "I'll have a surprise for her she when she gets back."

"A bridge-builder?" she said. She couldn't help but sound condescending.

"Something we have together," he said. "Something between her and me."

Finishing work the next day, he searched the woods well after dark, carrying crackers and peanuts and grapes. The two stuffed animals waited for him in the cab of the truck. When he failed to find the monkey, he came again the next evening, and the next. Sometimes he stopped and imagined himself a statue, an inanimate, stone idol, so still that the secret world around him couldn't help but make itself known through its movements. He often hunkered down in the undergrowth, motionless, and scanned for the white of the monkey's small, round face, its dark eyes and nimble jumps. Sometimes he thought he caught a glimpse of it. Other times he thought he saw Mary running through the trees.

At night, he lay in his bed examining the alligator and monkey. Somewhere along the line he had begun to think of himself as the reptile and Alyssa as a nimble, long-limbed, cute little ape with its incredible dexterity. It was like he was a small child again, imbuing these figures with lives of their own. Maybe they were looking for Mary together. He sometimes purposely blurred his eyes, trying to blend the face of the monster and the monkey in the dark. Silly, he knew, but he thought of it as his own kind of training, learning to visualize faces, Mary's features, as if by recreating her salient characteristics he could summon her from across the earth at his leisure. Weeks passed. Mary and Alyssa flew away.

A month, then two. He continued to search. He set humane traps but caught only raccoons. In late December he found what he believed to be evidence of the monkey's feeding, an empty bag of jelly beans that looked as if it had been clawed open and left in the branch of a tree. He tried calling Mary to give her the update. He got their housekeeper in Taiwan. "Tell her I'll call tomorrow," he said. "Are you writing this down?" The woman's stilted English sounded like a machine shaking itself apart. He couldn't tell if she was transcribing or conducting other housework. "Tell her I'm still working on getting a special something for her. She'll know what it means." He spent another ten minutes trying to make sure the message had been worded properly. His phone was charged fifty-seven dollars. Feeling unsatisfied, he relayed his progress to the two stuffed animals. They were passive, but seemed pleased, even hopeful.

He developed new methods, tied bananas halfway up trees only to have birds peck the skins to bits. Snow began to fall. The entire world became as white as the monkey's face. In the evenings, when he went out he saw in every hollow, every knot and rock and wind-kicked drift, a scampering and playful being just outside his reach. Sometimes he saw the monkey. Sometimes Mary. He stayed longer each night, sure it was only a matter of perseverance. He continued his method of hunkering in the underbrush, sitting in a single place for extended periods of time. When he slowed his breathing and rested his back against a tree, he could sense a larger secret hidden in the stillness, a way of seeing or understanding. Maybe this was the way Alyssa saw the world. Maybe it was the way of statues and dolls.

With the new year, a brief article highlighting Alyssa's move to Taiwan appeared in *ArtForum*. There was a mention of Alyssa, Mary, and the robot statues, but no photograph.

He worked during the day. He searched in the evening.

Finally, he began staying whole nights in the woods, always without shelter, always unmoving, like a bit of stone jutting up out of the terrain. Snowflakes fell about him in clumpy, wet layers, endlessly and silently altering the landscape so its features were reduced to their most obvious facets. The slope of a hill. A moss-protected rockface spicular with icicles. A fallen oak resting beneath the whiteness, its tendriled roots clasping at nothing. Some time in late January, on the coldest night yet, he watched for the thousandth time the sycamore where he'd first seen the monkey. The pale of the tree's bark was lost in the pale of the clinging and falling snow. His breath escaped in a heavy fog. Ice on ice. An indelible white on white.

Here monkey-monkey, he thought. Hours passed. His bones became rooted to the ground. Then in the sycamore in exactly the place he'd spotted it before, it appeared. Its small, black eyes burning a depth into the whiteness so that even from a hundred yards away, he could tell it was considering him. He wondered how Mary might depict that face in statue for them to look at forever. "Come on," he whispered. "You and me. We know each other." His body rattled, stirring itself into a shiver, but he pressed down the urge to move, allowed the cold to still him, to take over and do its job of keeping him concealed. Don't spook it, he thought. The monkey leaned out into space, its small hand clutching the branch. Then its fingers released, and for one horrible moment it looked as if it would plummet to the earth. But its body, limber, caught the end of a pine bough, dropped ten feet, swung down to the next, rebounded off the sycamore, zigzagged mid-air, shaking the whiteness from frond upon green frond, until the monkey splashed down into the silent snow.

"Here monkey-monkey," he said. He couldn't move without considerable pain, so he let the monkey come to him. The cold was in his skull. I'm the statue, he thought not for the first time.

A moment later the monkey was before him, hiking its legs up to tromp through the snow and look up into his face.

"I'm here," he whispered, "I'm waiting," and allowed it to draw near. "How have you survived this long?"

A rush of snow churned up by the wind momentarily blinded

him. He blinked, and the monkey was breathing in his ear. The weight of it was like he'd remembered. Its face like he remembered. Its smell and heat like he remembered.

"She'll be so happy to see you again," he said. "So happy."

As he said this he made out movement in the snowy distance. A prone and monstrous body was slithering toward him through the thicket. The sun had set long before, and at first the animal appeared only as a shadow, a trick of moonlight playing across the dead plants sticking up from the drifts. Then it worked its massive bulk around the base of the sycamore. The ancient thing with its gargantuan and scaly girth gained momentum, sliding forward on its great belly. Tom could hear twigs snapping under its weight, the crisp bone-like breaking muted by snowcover. He could also hear the thing breathing, the shuffling whisper as it paddled its way slowly through the snow. And just as it reached him, as he thought of his darling Mary, his beautiful Alyssa, as he pictured them all together, he saw too the monster at his feet, its jaws slowly opening as if in a grin.

GRACILE

GRACILE. AN ESOTERIC WORD, CERTAINLY. A THESAURUS WORD if ever there were one.

Gloria is gracile. Slender, small, compact. A gold pixie haircut and tanned cheeks. Twenty-two and suffering from recent disappointments reaped from a year abroad interning in Tanzania at the Jane Goodall Institute. Twenty-two, graduated with a biology degree, specialization in zoological sciences, with an interest in primates. Seven months in Dar es Salaam, four near Mount Kilimanjaro, and she's back in the States no richer or more employable. She does a stint delivering Jimmy John's sandwiches to kids at Ohio State, old classmates, before she finally lands an interview with the Columbus Zoo to clean bonobo cages.

She shows up at a cinder-block building behind the African Forest region. On the other side of an old metal desk sits a man named Allen, late fifties, director of the animal care staff. It's hot July and humid as anywhere she ever worked in Africa. They're in a sort of triage area for paperwork, not a real office, but a concrete room outside the offices with only a window high up in the wall and a screen door to let in the breeze. Gloria thinks she might pass out. She's so nervous. She's sweating. She's attempted to dress mildly zookeeper-ish—shorts and hiking boots, white button-up top.

"You'd be working with *Pan paniscus*," Allen says, his graying moustache tinted with the rusty color of tobacco. "Bonobos, to most people, aren't distinguishable from chimpanzees. Scientists thought they *were* chimpanzees for the longest time, till about '28. Guy named Coolidge actually discovered they weren't. Don't let anybody tell you it was Schwarz."

She doesn't know what he's talking about, but she nods: Okay. I'll remember that.

"What I mean is, because they were chimpanzees for so long,

people couldn't give up on the name. The bonobo had to be a version of the chimpanzee. People called them pygmy chimps. Or gracile chimpanzees."

He looks her over. "It means thin. Like you. You're gracile."

He reaches across and pats her hands. She doesn't know how to take this. His fingers linger. "They're built differently, the bonobos."

He finally leans back and looks at the ceiling. "They get to me."

He hires her. She's assigned the most menial duties, collecting trash, sweeping the walkway where people peer through the glass on the bonobo habitat. In the cages, she shovels feces. She hauls the manure out to barrels. It's taken away to be processed and sold as fertilizer somewhere in northern Ohio. She also xeroxes schematics of the habitat that highlight problem areas in the vegetation; she files requisitions for playground equipment from a custom manufacturing company in San Diego. She does everything but interact with the animals.

The first few months she searches her old haunts like a ghost who's forgotten she passed away. She flits about the bar scene she knew from college. The Library, Bernie's, Chumley's, a swilling, sticky barrage of bodies and smiles. She cradles a drink, sips and stares, but finds no one she knows. In a single short year all her closest friends have moved on. Her parents, who used to live less than ten miles from here, in Bexley, sold the optometry practice and retired early. They paint and read poetry in Flagstaff now.

Over the phone she tells her mother she's having trouble keeping up with the bills.

"Maybe you underestimated how nice it was," her mother says, "bringing your laundry over on the weekends. Having a place to stay during the summer."

"I just need to get ahead. If I can get a little ahead, I'll be fine."

"We can't send you money. We're all tied up."

"I didn't ask."

"We could send you a plane ticket. Move in with us?"

"I'm not leaving. This a good job opportunity."

"Shoveling poop?"

She tells her mother there's someone on the other line.

Nights after work, she passes the hospital on her way home. She sometimes stops and wonders which floor the babies are on. It's not motherhood or wifehood. Honestly, she can't really imagine those things. It's more the idea of a group—a collection of individuals to which you belong. In bonobos, it's called a 'party.' She likes that.

Had events gone differently, a certain man might have already been a member of her party. His name was Elvis Leon Montgomery, no lie. At an international fair at the Dar es Salaam University, he introduced himself in Kiswahili, though he was American. He had a rounded and boyish-looking face. He told her he'd come to meet other Americans, maybe even girls. He thought a salutation in the local language might impress them. She said it had.

After that, they spoke over the phone for two weeks. He'd gone to a technical school in Mississippi, but was smarter than that fact implied. She told him so. He'd answered an ad that touted international travel, and he worked as a diesel mechanic at an opencast mine on dumptrucks, nearly eight hundred of them. Despite transportation issues and scant time off, he borrowed a shiny blue Toyota from his supervisor. He drove from Geita to see her twice. They ate dinner and later they embraced in her apartment, though they drew the line at sex and kept their clothes on, feeling giddy and deliciously unsatisfied by the time he drove back in the mornings. The promise of more was close.

A month later, they both traveled with a small group which had been gathered by the UN and a sister university in the States, for a visit to Jane Goodall's old house at Gombe on Lake Tanganyika. She and Elvis walked along the muddy shore holding hands. As they explored the ugly beach together—despite having known each other so little time—she insisted he give up his job.

His work, she said, went against her principles.

"I don't know about that," he said.

She didn't know either, didn't have environmental impact

studies or know the effects of gold mining on local populations, soil erosion, animal habitats. But it certainly couldn't be good, any of it. She expressed this to him again on their long trip back across the placid waters. He responded half-heartedly, then looked away at the lush growth skirting the shoreline as if searching for wildlife amid the trees.

They didn't see each other after that. Maybe he feared the commitment. Or perhaps she'd given him the wrong impression, suggested in some way that her demand was unequivocal. She tried contacting him, to tell him she wasn't above reason. She'd be willing to work past such a chasm in their worldviews. Maybe this made her weak, she thought, that she was capable of chucking her personal convictions for a chance at romance, but she didn't much care. The loneliness she'd felt in this foreign country was tripled by his absence. And not all debates relied on the black versus the white. There was always the gray. The wrong impression, she thought. Thought it over and over. I've given the wrong impression and now am paying for it.

She traveled to Moshi for a different assignment. She let her new tasks take over to fill up her days. She told herself Elvis was a ridiculous name.

Now driving past the hospital she feels like that was her one shot at love. Stupid, right? She's twenty-two. Twenty-two! Smart, she thinks. Pretty. Career-minded. Knowledgeable and tough. World-traveled. Her whole life ahead of her.

But what about this bundle of desire in her stomach? Why stare at a hospital and wonder about a room full of newborns? Why crave a family so badly when your whole life lies ahead?

Irrational, she thinks. And yes. Elvis is most assuredly a ridiculous name.

Most days she arrives at the zoo about nine and doesn't emerge until six in the evening. The entire time she's immersed in a full-bodied funk. Her clothes are never free of the stink, even after several washings in the ultra-strength Tide she picked up her first day on the job. The smell is deepest in the cages, in the straw and pears, the apples, the half-eaten stems, the mangled browse, the pellets of monkey chow, and where the plucked black fur collects in the corners. After a few weeks, she quits resisting the odor. It happens in an instant. As if a switch is thrown. She embraces the overpowering effluvium of the bonobos, draws it deep into her lungs.

She thinks, This is me. This is my life.

The moment she accepts the scent, she feels a bottomless and abiding love for them all—all twenty-five bonobos, black-bodied, stretching, rolling, climbing, jumping, chattering. She begins to see the poetry in each of their names, how the letters circumscribe their faces. Kanzi, sound of a broken twig thrown into the water, the notched scar between his eyes pallid and pink. Nyota, the stubborn one. Sheldon, who loves television—every afternoon it's *Dora the Explorer* in the behavioral observation room. But most of all she loves Unga. Unga's bottom lip curving U-like—Uuuuuunga, Gloria thinks.

Gloria has watched Unga for weeks. Unga is about to be a mother. She's grown heavy-chested and languid as the due date draws near. The staff, the visitors, the media, are all on edge. Then one Wednesday, Unga is whisked away into a private enclosure where she's made off limits to all but select staff. Immediately there is speculation. She isn't seen for days. This is unusual.

By the following Friday, Unga has become a topic of gossip. Channel 4 Nightly News begins a segment called 'Baby Watch.' They show old footage of Unga over and over again. Visitors crowd the primate habitats looking for a glimpse. Speculation abounds.

This air of expectancy begins to infect the staff. Gloria goes about her duties with a distracted air. She ruminates over Unga as she hauls trash leaking soda and popcorn to the dumpster. Her mop in the restroom makes slow circles over the tiles as she tries to imagine Unga's thoughts, her unaccustomed isolation, her loneliness.

What is happening to Unga right now? There are rumors there was a complication with the birth, that Unga died. Rumors that the child died, that the zoo officials are waiting until after July 4th weekend to break the news of the tragedy.

Another week goes by and still no word.

Sometimes Gloria touches the outer wall of the building where she believes Unga still lies hidden inside.

At night she drives home and falls asleep in her little apartment off Eighth Avenue. In her lightless room, in an old brick house, she feels more alone than she ever has in her life.

Eminent visitors arrive at the zoo: two primatologists from Georgia drawling and conversing in voices like hot rubber. A veterinary specialist and a PR man from a sanctuary in Kinshasa. The whole complex crackles with life. More rumors. Unga is alive. The birth is quite near. Gloria hears the excitement bouncing off the stone walls of the inner observation rooms. She finishes her duties for the day and hangs about, a broom in her hand, in the break room, hoping for word. She hopes the broom will keep people from realizing she's off the clock.

Finally, late in the day, the group allowed access to Unga spills into the room for Coke and Cheetos. The staff veterinarian, Dr. Gabon, with her brilliant red curls, is sweating from her upper lip. She wipes it repeatedly. "Unga is taking her sweet time," she says.

"It's a special one, I think," the PR man replies.

"Special," says the Georgia primatologist. "How so?"

The PR man thinks hard. English is not his first language. "This time seems special to me. Is all I say."

They file out and down the hall. Unga is giving birth surrounded by strangers, and for some reason this gives Gloria a feeling of immense sadness, a feeling both gut-hollowing and heavy at the same time. She sits down, waiting, holding her broom across her lap like it's a safety bar on an especially scary roller coaster. She continues to wait. She doesn't know if she'll get in trouble for this, but she waits all the same.

Outside the air finally cools. The long shadows beneath the trees melt into a featureless gloom. The bonobos are brought in for the night. They grip at handfuls of straw before rolling over and trying to sleep. Occasionally Gloria hears them moving in their swings. Their normally drowsy boredom is charged with a restive and anxious energy. Down the hall is the occasional punctuation of a voice, a nervous laugh or snippet of instruction. Someone in sea-foam scrubs swishes by in slippered feet.

A few hours pass. The energy-saver light in the break room goes dark, and Gloria sits very still so as not to trigger it again. The darkness lends a volume to the sounds.

Then the wailing begins. In the dark, it's like a poltergeist howling down the corridor. More people rush by. Commands echo back and forth. More scrambling. Surgical tools clatter, fall to the floor, are recovered. Dr. Gabon chides someone, demands quiet.

And then there is. Quiet. It's a quiet to last a decade or a century or millennia. Gloria feels it, heavy and dense, teeming with living layers, this unsettling quiet. It appears no one is coming back. Gloria slips out slowly—so slowly the light doesn't come on.

In the silence of her apartment she lies on her bed and stares at the ceiling. The howling from the birthing room chases her into sleep. Horrible visions populate her dreams. Unga splayed out on an operating table, her organs exposed, a human baby sitting up in the middle of them and playing with the kidney and spleen like they were toys.

The phone rings. She answers, and on the other end is a man. "Is this Gloria?"

"Yes." She sits up, straightens her hair.

"Gloria, I'm Chet Quincy."

"Sounds like a superhero's secret identity," she says.

He laughs an easy laugh. "I like that. Sorry to bother you at this hour—"

"You're not," she says. "Bothering me. I'm completely free."

She doesn't know Chet Quincy from a mud puddle. But his voice is handsome and strong-jawed, sun-kissed with deep bravado.

"Good, good," he says. "The reason I'm calling is I'm a reporter with The Columbus Dispatch. I'd like to do a story on you."

"A story?" she says.

"Human interest. Hometown girl makes good. Nothing major. No headlines." He laughs again, light as hydrogen. "You went to Africa, right? Now you're working with the monkeys?"

She should correct him, say 'primates.' "I went to Tanzania," she says. "I work—" She hesitates. "With Bonobos."

"Sure," he says. "Sounds good. All that sounds interesting enough. Can I interview you, maybe tomorrow night?"

"They're the gracile chimpanzees," she says. "And yes. Yes, you can."

Crowds flow into the zoo, the rumor mill begins its daily grind, and news vans linger at the edge of the parking lot. The primate complex where Unga is held sits silent. Gloria conducts her work. She tries to focus on her upcoming meeting with Chet Quincy. She rehearses the important and interesting facts about her travels: the Bantu word for friend; historical tidbits about Zanzibar; a study she'd read, which had made the rounds at the institute, about the generosity of bonobos; the taste of Nigerian bitter leaf.

All that day the eminent visitors and administrative staff are nowhere to be found. Gloria sees Allen only once, traversing the halls at a speedy clip. He holds a cell phone tight to his ear and says, "I understand." Then he disappears into the inner sanctum and doesn't emerge again until evening as Gloria is leaving. He's smoking a cigarette beneath the eaves where a scraggly copse of bamboo creates an alcove. He motions for her to come over.

"What is it?" she says. "I have to meet someone."

"I know you want to see Unga."

"Don't say that," she says. "Don't tease." But she smiles at hearing Unga's name.

"You haven't heard," he says.

"Is Unga okay?"

"It's not Unga," he says. "The baby's deformed. It has wings."

She steps back. "Stop it. That's not funny."

"I'm not being funny. They didn't see it on the ultrasound because the wings were folded over the shoulder blades."

"I don't understand."

"What's to understand," he says. "A primate with wings. Do you want to see or not?"

She doesn't know how to respond. This feels like blackmail or a trap. "I can see her?"

"If you want. You can owe me."

He leads her back through the complex. The large crowds have been cleared out by security. Even the staff are mostly gone. Night feels heavy around them. They pass the break room. At the end of a long, block hallway is a steel door with a small observation window reinforced with chickenwire. Allen pulls a key card from his pocket and swipes it, producing a high-pitched click in the lock. He places a finger in front of his mouth.

A small anteroom runs the length of the observation pen. They're separated by a wall of heavy plexiglas. Crescentic reflections from the orange bulbs make half-halos that hang in the air between them and Unga.

When Gloria sees her, she gasps in delight. Unga is alive and well. The drowsy female lies in a soft heap of straw piled up in the corner of an open green cage. Above her are heavy ropes criss-crossing from one corner to the next, a tire swing frozen in place, not a hint of movement. And there in Unga's arms is the baby.

"It's a girl," Allen says.

The baby's bright eyes are open, a shock of deep black hair gathered at the top of her head. She's so small. So very small—the size of a human newborn or slighter. She's staring up at them, at Allen and Gloria, as she suckles. Her elfin hand reaches for them.

"She likes you," Allen whispers.

The baby tilts its head, extends its arm.

A rising warmth in Gloria's chest, fluid and faint, suddenly boils up and becomes a flood that spills over and runs through all her limbs. She feels a love for this child swelling from somewhere infinite and mystifying.

"Why are you showing me this?" she says.

"Because I've always liked you," he says. "And she won't be here long. They've kept her hidden. They're waiting."

"For what?"

"The anniversary of *The Wizard of Oz*."

Gloria turns away from the child to stare at Allen. "What do you mean? What does that have to do with anything?"

"August twenty-fifth," he says, "is only a few weeks away. That's the day in 1939 the movie was released nationally. They want to fly her to San Diego and do a whole tie-in. Flying monkeys and all. Then cross the country on a tour back to Columbus." He nods toward mother and child. "Of course, Unga would go, too."

The baby releases its latch on its mother and leans out over the straw. Unga lets it fall forward gently, and Gloria for the first time sees the baby's wings, the gray-skinned, almost batlike curvature of two extra appendages sprouting from either side of its spine high up on the back. As it struggles to right itself, the wings rise like a bird's just before liftoff.

Gloria takes deep, irregular breaths. The wings part further, and Gloria touches the glass. The child pushes up. Its wings are feebly held out the way a man's arms on a highwire are extended for balance. The wings look hardly useful for flying, yet they're oddly adept.

"I still don't understand," Gloria says.

"Like I said: what's to understand? A primate with wings is good publicity. Kismet. It should line up with the seventy-fifth anniversary of the movie. Good press for re-releases, Blu-Rays or whatever. Good press for bonobos."

"You can't do that," Gloria says. "People will get the wrong impression. They'll misinterpret. The flying monkeys were bad."

He laughs at that. It sounds ridiculous to her, too, what she just said.

The baby looks again at Gloria. Never in all her time amid primates has Gloria felt the way she does now. She loves this baby. Loves it, and knows she'll never be able to get away from that love. She can't rectify the thought of it with the flying minions of the Wicked Witch of the West. Will the PR people dress it in a red-striped jacket and cap? Will children learn to revile it?

"Her name is Dorothy, if that helps," Allen says.

"They'll get the wrong impression," she says again.

Dorothy, the wobbling baby girl in the hay with its wings quivering, reaches out for Gloria.

"You see what I mean," Allen says. "Practically human." He moves closer to Gloria. "Gracile. Like you." He places his cold, rough hand on her lower back, reaches around her hips, and draws her close. A part of her, still in awe of the child, doesn't register this as it happens. Allen kisses her neck, and her body is seized with terror or collapse. She turns into him and pushes his chest, but he holds her.

"Now stop that," he says. "Stop it. Just give in a little. It'll be nice." He pulls her toward him.

She tries kneeing him in the groin, but he twists to the side.

"Just one," he says.

Out of the corner of her eye, she detects a black shape flying through the air. It's a blur, quick, something akin to a ball tossed by a child. Allen must see it too because he stops. He turns his head. "Did you see that?" Gloria rears back and head-butts him. It isn't clean; her forehead strikes his cheek, but he lets go.

"Ow, God!" he says.

They separate, standing apart, breathing heavily. Gloria shudders, focusing with every stitch of her resolve on not passing out. She feels woozy from the headbutt.

"I'm sorry," Allen says. "I don't—I don't know what that was." He feels his nose, his cheek, finds no blood.

"This is bad, isn't it?" he says.

"I've given you the wrong impression," she says. She hears the air moving through her nose, feels the vibration as her breath barrels down her trachea. There's the smell again, the whole-bodied scent of the bonobos lingering in the room, traveling through her, swimming in and out of her body. It's like breathing dirt. Her vision dribbles down to a pinhole in which she sees Allen looking frightened and old.

Breathe, she tells herself.

She pulls it in, all that heavy air, finds strength in it.

"I have to meet someone," she says. She picks up Allen's key card from the counter. He doesn't try to stop her. He's looking into the cage at Unga and the baby.

"Did you see?" he says behind her. Gloria opens the door. "Did you see that? Did you see it?"

Driving in the dark along a highway skirted with harsh-looking trees, she tries to shake the adrenaline and fear out of her muscles. Her hands defy the command from her brain. Her fingers spasm and jerk and flutter. The headlights roll from one side to the other as she struggles to stay between the lines. Every few minutes she picks up her phone from the passenger seat, dials 9-1-1, then deletes each number slowly and drops the phone with a soft thud.

She arrives in German Village feeling exhausted. She parks along a row of quaintly refurbished brick buildings, now a bookstore, a restaurant. People walk the streets in quiet twos, threes, fours, ducking into bars with spellbinding neons coiled in quiet windows. She's safe here. Was she ever not? The moment at the zoo seems remote, almost unimportant. She tells herself, yes, unimportant— only because the memory's been crowded out by the baby. Dorothy. Had she seen what she thought she saw?

She commands her hand to open the door. She commands her legs to lift her out of the seat. She meets Chet Quincy at a cafe. He's tall, a tad thin, with straw-colored hair. He wears turtleshell glasses and fashionable shoes. He smiles like he knows he's handsome.

"It's good to meet you," he says.

"Likewise." They shake hands. Hers is still trembling, but he doesn't comment. They go inside, order a drink for which he pays, and find a seat. They're practically alone in a quiet corner while outside more people pass by.

"Your life must be pretty intriguing," he says. "Let's start with your education."

"I want to get this out there," she says. She's still thinking about Dorothy, about Allen, but pushes these to the annex of her mind. "I want you to know, I'm nothing. I'm a glorified shoveler of shit."

He flinches as if he isn't used to hearing bad language.

"I don't mean," she says, "to sound ungrateful, or jaded. I just want you to know you're talking to a nobody, really. I'm the lowest at the zoo. I'm a janitor. Just to be honest." Part of her wishes she weren't telling Chet Quincy these things, but she hates the thought he's been misled. She wants desperately to start on the right foot, for him not to get the wrong impression.

"Oh," he says. He sets down his pen, which he's been holding over a small note pad. "But you do have access, right? To the bonobos?"

"Access," she says, and feels for Allen's key card in her pocket.

"I mean, you can see them when you want."

"I can get into the complex, if that's what you mean."

He smiles. "Don't worry. This is a small piece. You're at the beginning of your career. We'll go with a rising-star theme. You'll sound great. It won't be a lie. It'll be something people read between the pages of war, death, and destruction. People want optimism. They want to know good things are happening."

He smiles again and touches the pen to paper.

"Good things," she repeats.

The interview starts off well and he suggests they graduate from coffee to dinner at a bistro only a few blocks away. The restaurant specializes in a nebulous mix of world cuisine. He seems to know the maître d', a tall woman with long fingers. She seats them at a table near the patio where the night air rolls in sweet and heavy. A wine list appears, disappears, is conjured into a stately, dark bottle with an unflashy label.

They talk for nearly two hours. She begins to lose the fear still lingering in her body. Her adrenaline drains away, leaving only a solid sense of outrage.

But even her anger begins to soften with the second bottle of wine. Chet Quincy asks her questions about Africa, about her associations with the universities and international foundations. He asks for names, particularly African names of places, which he says add flavor to the page. "They're pepper," he says. He even inquires about her friendships, her personal life. She hints at a romance that didn't play out so well, but stops before it sounds tragic.

"Just something that didn't go anywhere," she says.

He nods. "What about working with the animals? Any good stories? Anecdotes?"

She thinks of Dorothy sitting up, her wings outspread. "I tend to their habitat," she says. "I'm sorry. I'm so boring."

"Don't be that way. You're not boring. For instance, I bet you know something about Unga."

A sliver of unease skitters up her spine. Hairs rise on the back of her neck.

"There's word," he says, "that something's wrong with the baby."

She begins to stand. "I'm not your story," she says. "I see that."

"Whoa whoa," he says. "Look, I'm just asking. We're hitting it off. I don't want to jeopardize that. If you want to tell me about Unga, that's okay. If not, that's okay, too. All on the up and up. You don't want to say anything about the monkeys, I'm still paying for the meal."

"They're primates," she says.

"Primates," he repeats. "See. I'm learning already."

He smiles again, runs his hand down her arm. And because she can't bear to think of going home, she sits. She sits because letting her mind wander in the dark of her bedroom, with no one to talk to about what's happened today, feels like it might be the absolute worst, and she just wants a little company for a little while longer.

"Her name's Dorothy," she says.

"The infant, the baby bonobo?"

"Yes."

"I heard," he says, glancing about the room, "there's a deformity."

"Who told you that?"

"I have sources." He's smiling, and there might be something between them now. She wants it to be. If she just gives in, there will be. She's sure of it. He and she will start on the right foot, no wrong impressions. Her loneliness will shatter.

He refills her wine glass. She feels giggly, free of the constricting fear she's felt all evening. Her anxiety is absolutely dissipating. She picks up the glass and drinks deeply.

"It has wings," she whispers.

"Wings? Oh, come on. That's not funny."

"I'm serious."

He grins. "I get it. You don't have to tell me."

She stands, feeling reckless and light, like a wild bird borne up on high winds.

"Get us another bottle of wine," she says. "We'll take it with us."

There's no security in the back parking lot this time of night. She squeezes through the broken gate with no trouble. She's gracile, after all—small, compact. He struggles to follow and tears his shirt, but finally stands before her, holding up the new bottle of wine and two plastic cups. He's disheveled, and she pokes his exposed stomach. He doubles over with quiet and half-drunken laughter. She holds a hand to her mouth.

"You have to be very quiet," she says.

He wrestles the pre-extracted cork from the bottle's neck and pours heavily. They drink and move through the darkness, avoiding the illuminated areas, sticking to the shadows. It all feels so very freeing. Dangerous without being criminal. They're not hurting anyone, she thinks. Plus, she deserves this. A little fun.

She uses the swipe-card to let them into the ape habitat. She's surprised there are no guards. No one. Just quiet.

Swaddled in Unga's embrace is the baby. Its black, hirsute face, is peaceful against her left bicep. Its eyes flicker beneath the lids.

"She's dreaming," Gloria says.

"What a beautiful picture," he says. He's swaying less now, his posture more rigid. "Can I take one? A picture?"

She hesitates, but he's doing it already with his phone. She lets him. He lifts a few scrawled pages off the table. Other field notes and bureaucratic-looking paperwork lie about as if someone has only stepped out for a moment.

"We need to go," she says.

"In a minute. Listen to this." He reads from the file. "'Superfluous flaps of skin, cartilage and some evidence of meekly developed muscle. A doubling of the scapula connected by fibrous sinew as an extension of the trapezoid ligament. This ligament, extending over the superior notch, creates, for lack of a better term, a wing.' That's so wild."

He keeps riffling through the papers and tries logging onto a laptop with no luck.

"We should go," she says.

He discovers a printed email pinned beneath the laptop. He reads it silently. Feeling lightheaded, she draws closer to him and sees mention of San Diego, the words "Wizard of Oz" and "tour."

"This is better than I ever could have hoped," he says. He takes pictures of it all. She half-heartedly bats at his hands.

"You can't," she says, "I'll get in trouble," but even to her own ears she lacks conviction. She sits down in a nearby plastic chair. The room spins. "You gave me the wrong impression," she says.

He finishes taking a few more pictures of the mother and child. "I deeply appreciate everything." He actually salutes her, then pats her on the shoulder and exits the room.

A flash-charged media storm thunders on the horizon. Zoo officials and Warner Brothers marketing mavens huddle in board rooms and pencil out itineraries. Design firms, with blistering swiftness, sketch model entranceways in a palette of pre-determined greens associated with the Emerald City. Ticket sales are calculated. Box office revenues from the based-on-a-true story summer release next year glow at the end of a long tunnel constructed of hype, relatable characters, and at least one instance of dire circumstances and fortitude parlayed into finale gold. Adaptations—cartoons and theatrical re-imaginings with fanciful backstories—piggyback the film's success.

She sees it, this surrounding tempest of endless coverage, charging its way into her world, threatening to batter and toss her far from its center, far from Unga and Dorothy, and again into the vastness of her own solitude. To her mind, Dorothy, the baby, is more than the sum of her promotional potential. She's a being born of loneliness. Why have wings if you don't mean to fly away?

Without much more thought, she opens the cage and holds her hand out to Unga, who takes it. It's the first time she's touched one of them. The palm and meat of the fingers are leathery cool. Dorothy is scooped up into Unga's arms, and the three of them trundle out into the night. Where she's going, she can't say.

The night slithers cold against her skin as they exit the primate house.

Allen is waiting, fifteen feet from the entrance, as if he's been camped here, waiting for this moment. His arm is held on his hip at an angle that makes him appear broken. Gloria's stomach trembles. Without stepping toward her, he opens his hands, spreads his arms like a man showing he's unarmed.

"I'm real sorry," he says. His voice is soft and shallow. It makes him as old as he is, which for the first time she notices is not a man in his late fifties, as she orignally thought, but perhaps somewhere in his mid-sixties, maybe even pushing seventy.

"I couldn't go home," he says. "I've been thinking about what I did all night."

She shields Unga and Dorothy. "Don't come over here."

"I wanted you to know," he says. "I'm lonely. I'm old and I'm lonely. A widower, not that I want your pity. I'm an idiot, too. Sometimes I see you, I think you've got it all, everything." He hesitates, then begins to weep, not trying to hide it. Silvery tears tumble down his cheeks. "I can't lose this job," he says. "I don't have what you have."

She's so stunned, she forgets her fear. "What do I have? What do you think I have?"

"You have everything." He sweeps his arm out, signaling toward the sky. "You have your future."

"We're leaving," she says.

He stares at her, hangdog and jowly, his limp moustache ridiculously cartoonish. "I can't let that happen. I couldn't let you leave, not with them."

"I'll go," she says. "I'll call the police."

Those ridiculous tears still rolling, still dripping onto his sad paunch, he says, "You should probably do that. You should. I won't tell them any different if you do. I understand. But I can't let you take my girls."

Unga slips her handhold. She lopes around Gloria toward Allen. He crouches on the balls of his feet and opens his arms. Mother and child stop a foot away, sniff, then clutch at him. He stands, holding Unga, Unga holding Dorothy.

"This is the family I got dealt," he says, "and now they're leaving."

Gloria sees it now, that Allen isn't in the plans for Unga's travels. He won't be the one to watch over Dorothy. "It all goes away," he says, "We all get to the end of things. I know that, but I don't have to like it." He carries the heavy primate and her child toward the doors—a little party, Gloria thinks.

"I'm sorry," she hears herself say. "For you. I'm sorry you don't get to go."

He stops with the doors open and turns. "Tell me," he says. He's wiping his eyes. "Why'd you get into this business? The primates. What led you to them?"

She's not ready for the question. She's still trying to piece together what's happening right now. She'd envisioned for a moment herself and Unga and Dorothy on the road in her car, a screwy movie scene, which in this moment seems ridiculous and fantastic and not at all real. Tumbling slowly through her consciousness is the fact that she was committing a felony and that Allen stopped her.

"What did you say?" she says.

He hitches Unga higher on his hip. "I said, what led you here? What made you want to work with the bonobos? I never asked you that."

She recalls a moment, five years before, sitting in senior Spanish class with the teacher off somewhere, the malaise of late spring, the last high school rites fizzling like a cordite fuse approaching an explosive end—commencement jitters, pomp and circumstance, post-graduation parties in old barns, kids giggling over illicit beers and Jim Beam. Sitting in that Spanish class, she'd been daydreaming, imagining the future in a vague shadow-show of sex and love and easy chatter, easy smiles, friends and family. Then a sophomore girl stomped through the doorway. The girl was wheezing, her freckled face bitter red. "Brett Barry is dead," she said. "Brett Barry died." Then off like a moth released in the quiet. Kids stood. Kids dug for their phones. Kids furiously texted. Kids searched for an authority figure. Brett Barry dead in a car crash on the last week of school, skipping out the last few periods, running a stop sign and colliding with another vehicle. Brett Barry with his brother and two other juniors flung against a tree in a nearby yard, but only Brett Barry dead. Brett Barry, with his stupid name and his stupid laugh, dead and gone. Gloria had dated him freshman year for like a week, and all she could remember was he was crazy about monkeys. He wanted to work with monkeys or something. She thought about how Brett Barry never would have been smart enough to do that. Brett Barry was community-college material, she'd thought, associate degree, at best. That was the real Brett Barry, despite all the overly hospitable things people said about him later on. But in Spanish class, that was her moment. Did it matter who carried out a mission? Maybe dead Brett Barry's dream could be hers, and she found she liked the shape of it, the way Brett Barry's dumb dream fit her own. The way it opened an avenue through a pack of people, a little road where she might find meaning, and only now she's wondering if she were wrong.

Allen waits in the doorway with Unga and Dorothy.

"I guess," she says, "I always thought working with primates was a way to never be alone. They don't get the wrong impression about you."

He smiles a little. "It was a toy," he says. "A piece of a tire for the bonobos to play with. The thing I saw earlier, when we were standing in front of the cage. I thought it was Dorothy flying. Maybe there's been too much hype. Or I just wanted to believe it. But it was a toy. Unga threw a toy at us when she saw me grab you."

"Oh," she says meekly.

"That's the conclusion I came up with when I saw it: a flying monkey. Not the most reasonable answer. Despite knowing everything I know, being as old as I am, I believed it though. I thought it was a flying monkey, just for a second."

"Me too," she says. She wants to say something about how stupid that makes her feel, more false impressions, but he talks first.

"I think that's wonderful," he says. "Thinking something like that can still happen. It's wonderful. Even if it wasn't what we thought. It was a good thing. We believed in it for a little bit."

She regards him in the door, the sad light of the hallway behind him. She's unsure if she'll come back tomorrow. She hasn't worked it all out yet. But she's waiting now. Maybe, she thinks, Dorothy is waiting, too. For a moment in the moonlight, for a view of open sky. Before Allen carries her back inside, she'll spread her wings and go. She waits.

From somewhere in the zoo, the cattle egrets call back and forth, their rickety laughs rolling rustily and machine-like. Dorothy raises her head off Unga's shoulder, and for an instant, all three of them, Dorothy, Unga, and Allen, are listening to whatever comes next, to the moon, to Gloria. Really listening.

"I'm lonely, too," Gloria says, so low she doesn't know if she's been heard. "I'm lonely, and I want magic, something magical to happen. I need it."

"We all want that," he says. "It's why we're all waiting."

"Waiting?" she says. "For what?"

Allen dusts some straw away from Unga's fur. He nods toward Dorothy but never takes his eyes off Gloria. "We're waiting to see what she does next," he says. "Because no matter what, it'll be exciting."

He smiles again, a lost, shabby sort of look to him, and for a moment she forgives him his transgressions because she's the one, the world quaking beneath her feet, the open air trembling, she's the one waiting, breathless, strong, alone but suddenly buoyant, fierce and expectant for the unsung future.

"We did see her fly," she says.

"What?"

"Tonight, we saw her fly. It's why we have to go. We're the ones who got her to fly."

His mouth slides upward, a smile. "We've been working with her," he says. "We're vital."

"They couldn't do without us," she says.

"Because they want to believe."

"In something," she says. "It's okay, because we all need it."

"The magic," he says.

"Hope," she says.

"Family."

Standing there, she sees herself anew. Twenty-two, she thinks. Twenty-two and the world ahead of me. She holds out her arms just as a test. To see if Dorothy might fly to her.

Bring it on, she thinks. Bring it on, I'm ready.

TRACKING

DURING THE CIVIL RIGHTS MOVEMENT OF THE SIXTIES, HE WAS a lean and slightly awkward figure, blurred to a dull gray in the background of photographs, his limbs obscured by errant spray from the fire hoses used on protesters.

During the eighties, he sat with heads of state. I've found numerous images of a leg. An arm. Clad in a hue of blue that was fashionable at the time and may soon come into vogue again. These things are circular.

In the nineties, he switched professions and lifestyles altogether. His new milieu was the bush, the tree, the yard, the lattice, the rolling hills of landscaped lawns on wealthy estates. A broad-brimmed straw hat always obscured his eyes. His skin had darkened with constant exposure to the sun, so much so that I began to fear for him about maladies like melanoma, and even everyday sunburn. In many of these photos, highlighted as they are in certain magazines detailing the lifestyles of men and women with more money than anyone I know, he has adopted the easy air of a man who knows his place in the world and has finally accepted who he is. He looks healthy, and not just because he is lean. His posture is one of calm.

You may have wondered why I didn't mention the seventies. He was not around in the seventies, which is when I was born.

In the new millennium, sightings of him became and continue to become rarer. He is certainly older now, and his shifting from one profession to another doesn't lend itself to the kind of intense and narrow searching I used to do. I sometimes think I see him in an ad on a bus or as a mirage palimpsested on the back of a newspaper page, the sun shining through, giving me a sense of him on the other side.

The newest development I have to report is that I've begun, for the first time, to see him in person. Subways and taxis are always culprits, as they provide for fleetfooted getaway. At the corner of my eye, he appears, a gait I've imagined a million times over, a slight stoop to the way he jogs into traffic, hustling between the halted cars on Twelfth Avenue on his way to an appointment, a new job, a new home in a new part of the country. This development gives me hope, however. I've never been so close, and with the coming decade my father must certainly slow down, must certainly lose, as we all will lose, that step that's kept him ahead of me for so long.

DEPARTURES
AND ARRIVALS

PAL HESITATED AT THE EDGE OF THE PLATFORM, TESTING his balance. The train was a long way off—he couldn't hear it—and looking at the tracks below gave him a dizzy, nauseous feeling, the same helium bubble he felt in his stomach while looking out from the observation decks of very tall buildings.

"Stop that," his mother said. She pulled him away from the edge still speaking into her phone. "No, not you. It's Pal. Eight-year-olds. Especially boys. Always testing the limits, pushing your patience." She led him back to the bench and released his arm.

He wandered toward the edge again. His father had been gone nearly nine months. That's how long it took to make a baby. He knew that much. Maybe his father had been reincarnated as a woman's egg and was just now getting ready to pop his head through some lady's "downstairs area."

He imagined what his father might look like as a newborn. There'd be black hair certainly, and a prominent nose, even for a baby. The doctors would snip a purple, slimy cord. The doctor would smack his father's bare behind, which would make his father cry. That'd cinch it. He'd recognize his father's yowling because it'd be a baby version of what his father used to do in the bathroom, when he locked the door and ran the water and thought Pal didn't know he was in there. That'd be the thing. The crying.

Pal knew what newborns looked like because he'd seen them on television. His mother was forever watching shows about medical procedures, plastic surgeries, anatomical anomalies, births, deaths, and autopsies that seemed to make a mockery out of any sort of television rating system. You couldn't say *dick* or *pussy*—Remie had taught him those—on regular television, but you could show a real corpse's gray matter dribbling onto the sidewalk. This made him think of his father again.

He felt the edge of the platform beneath the arches of his feet. He turned to see if his mother were watching. She wasn't. She was still talking on the phone and staring at a poster of Daniel Craig. In addition to the gory, medical reality shows, his mother liked Daniel Craig. Pal knew that, too.

The terminal was empty. A few weeks ago, Pal had stood like this where the platform ended, pretending to be a man on a cliff. Below him, only a few feet down were the tracks. His mother hadn't been looking then either, but a fat man with the transportation authority had tromped over and grabbed him roughly by the shoulder. The man had scratched at his big, jowly neck as he marched Pal back to his mother. The man's eyes were wide with anger. He looked nothing like Pal's father, whose eyes were always sad. The man had given Pal's mother a few stern words, then walked away and disappeared into a door that said AUTHORIZED PERSONNEL.

Pal's mother had said, "What a grouch," then gone back to talking on the telephone.

Pal heard the train. It was sliding around a bend in the hill beyond the station, flowing like a silver snake out of the trees.

"I'll have to call you back," his mother said. She beckoned for Pal to come to her, to wait with her by the bench. "Daddy's going to be super surprised."

This was how it had gone nearly every day for nine months. At 4:15, he and she stood upright, holding hands, waiting on the crowds to alight and swell like riverwater blasting forth from a broken dam. Every afternoon, the two of them, like rocks with the fluid people and their expressionless faces sluicing past in a scuff-shoe shuffling and whisper of clothing.

It was only the first day that had been different. That day, she'd picked him up from school. His first day as second grader, in fact. It had been his mother's idea to meet his father at the terminal. "He'll just be getting off the train from work. It'll be a surprise," she said. "Would you like to go see your dad?"

Pal had shrugged. "Sure."

"And then get pizza?"

His face beamed. "Really?"

"Really. All three of us."

When they'd arrived, his father was already there. His father looked thin and his gray-checked suit hung on him. His red tie shot up in the wind and licked his face like a tongue. There was a crowd that day, people waiting to leave from a large church gathering across the street. His mother didn't see his father at first. Pal was about to point him out, but the local was just coming in. A big, glowing number was on its front: 5181, the train his father was supposed to be on. His mother stepped forward into the crowd, already searching the windows. People blocked Pal's view so that all he could see was the top of his father's head.

Then his father's black hair was gone, and a woman was screaming. The train stopped in a herky-jerky way. The people in the windows lurched forward. The woman kept screaming. People banged on the doors from inside the train. The doors swooshed open.

But that day the crowd didn't dissipate or turn to water. It oozed on to the platform in a single, slow mass. The commuters huddled together as if gelled to one another.

"Stay here," his mother said. She sat him on the bench. "Don't move." She waded into the throng. People began shouting, but no one ran, no one backed away, no one retreated from the train in panic. His mother returned, her face ashen.

"What happened?" Pal said.

She seemed not to know what to do with her hands. She ran them down her thighs, placed them on her mouth, then pushed her hair back from her forehead. "A man," she said. "Some poor man threw himself onto the tracks. He got run over by the train." Her hands dropped to her hips, then reached for Pal's shoulders.

"The man died," she said.

"Not daddy?"

"No no no," she said. "No, sweetie. It wasn't daddy. Daddy didn't get home on the train today. He's staying in the city. He's working late. We made a mistake." She pulled him from the train station, the two of them passing through the empty tunnel and up the stairs to the main street.

An ambulance arrived as they pulled away.

Now every day they waited. Nine months. She picked Pal up from school. They drove straight to the train terminal. His father did not arrive. "Guess it's the city again," she'd say. And the two of them went home for the night.

Nine months was a school year, too. He'd be finished with second grade soon. He wondered what would happen in the summer. It'd had been a year of learning—cursive and multiplication—but also a new and secret kind of education, of how to know and how to pretend not to know. When his mother that first night met the men at the front door, Pal had stayed in his room. She'd wept down there in the living room, more loudly than his father ever had in the bathroom. His mother hadn't yet learned how to keep her pain secret by running water to drown out the sound, to stifle her hiccups for air in a towel, or to wash away the moans that came from the gut by flushing the toilet. Even Pal knew how to do that. He'd learned from watching his father through the keyhole.

That night, the first time his father didn't come home, and after the men had visited their house and his mother cried in the living room, she'd entered his room. A waxy, unbroken smile kept her lips pinned against her teeth. Her cheeks had gone blotchy from strain.

"Daddy's not coming home tonight," she said.

"You already said that," he said.

"Oh. That's right." She leaned down and kissed his forehead. She opened her mouth but seemed to lose whatever words were about to slip out. Pal waited, but nothing came. A breeze tickled the curtains in his open window, and he imagined the words escaping into the night before she could say them.

She stood up straight. "So," she said, "we'll just have to pick him up tomorrow. Sound good?"

This was the beginning of his secret knowing. An unsaid body of understanding lay between him and her, on the floor at their feet. He could pick it up and shake it and hand it to her and make her see it, make her see that it was there and that he saw it too. But he also understood what this would do to her. How it might send them toppling into the crack in the floor made by that body of understanding, and how heavy the body would suddenly be. Heavy enough to drag them down to the center of the world where there was fire and molten rock roiling in lava pools. He'd learned that much in a science lesson and knew no people could live down there.

"Pizza?" he said.

"What?"

"Can we get pizza? All three of us?"

"Sure, baby. That'd be great."

Unlike his father, she hadn't hid in the downstairs bathroom. After the first day at the train station, she'd suddenly filled her time talking to other women on the telephone. She got in touch with old friends from high school. She helped plan events at a church she never attended. She ordered things, always over the phone, and always bland little housewares that cost more to ship than to purchase—a kitchen towel with a cross-stitched snowman in the center, scrub brushes, scented candles, tins of popcorn, a sheet set, and a small sign for the front door that said, "Dogs Welcome—Cats . . . Well, Cats are going to to do what they want anyway."

They'd never owned pets.

She spent hours with the customer service representatives deciding between blue or puce linens. And when she wasn't on the phone, she watched shows. The medical trauma shows came first. Ones with amazing tales of survival. A man mauled by an elephant who lived to tell about it. A woman who'd lost both ears to frostbite in the Yukon. Then to surgery shows, heroic doctors performing thirteen-hour surgeries to save premature twins, quick-thinking miners who'd stitched up wounds with thread from their jackets to survive their time trapped after a cave-in. When she stopped finding stories of survival, she moved on to anything medical, anything dealing with the human body. The gorier the better, and so Pal became quite familiar with the fragility of the flesh.

He tottered at the edge of the platform. Old local 5181 straightening out as it drew near. His mother called for him again.

He wondered now what would happen if he dove onto the tracks. He could imagine the way the steel would slice down through bone. He tried envisioning his own shoe lying near his body with the foot still in it. He thought about the unnatural way his arm might be turned, wrapped up his back and around his shoulder so it touched his ear from behind. He imagined his own face missing. His father's face. Missing.

He'd thought more about jumping in front of the train lately.

In the last nine months, on the days he didn't have school and their routine was broken, the air in the house felt like glass. These were the bad times, when school didn't provide them with a reason to swing by the station. 4:15 would come and go, and his mother would say nothing. On his days off from school, she wouldn't answer the phone or watch the television. Sometimes she looked at him funny as if she'd forgotten to mention something about his grades or dinner.

He didn't like her silent like that. Her hands started up with their pointless moving. They slid back and forth across the table or straightened antimacassars over and over again.

And summer stood only weeks away, a horrible mass of sunshine and schedule-less silence.

So he thought about jumping.

Train 5181 came closer. He could see the conductor now, a middle-aged woman in a dark, satin jacket. She was waving for Pal to move back. Her eyes were furious. She reached for the lever on the control panel.

Pal felt the nauseous feeling in his stomach again. Summer. His father. The train station over and over. His toes hovered above the tracks. Then his mother's hand was around his wrist. She led him away as the train glided and released its normal hisses and metallic shrieks.

They stood by the bench and waited.

"Summer is soon," he said.

The two of them looked toward the train as it came to a full stop. She was quiet as the people came through the doors. She always was. Always searching through the windows.

The people passed them by. He thought of jumping onto the tracks tomorrow or the next day. Summer was soon. Summer and all its horribleness. Nine months he'd persisted with her, pretended when pretending was almost more than he could bear. Even when the men came to tell her that her husband had not, in fact, worked for their company for three weeks before what they called the "accident." Pal's father had been let go. Budget cuts. The men were sorry to say this. Pal had pretended not to have heard, knowing if he addressed it, she'd still insist his father was in the city. She'd tell Pal that his father had taken a new job and that his schedule remained unchanged. "Some nights he stays in the city," she would say, undaunted. "We just want to make sure we're at the station to meet him if he makes it home."

Over and over.

The flow of people dribbled away so that they were left alone, still waiting by the bench.

"He must have decided to stay another night," she said.

"Summer is soon," Pal repeated.

"Sure is." She leaned down so that she was speaking with him face to face. "You looking forward to no homework?"

"We'll stop coming here," he said.

"Sure sure," she said. She acted as if she hadn't thought of it. "Doesn't make sense to come here if I'm not already picking you up. Let your dad find his own way home." She pointed herself toward the exit. This time Pal caught her hand.

"Mom," he said. "Can we wait for one more train tonight?"

"I don't see—"

"Dad might just be late. On the 6324." Nine months, Pal had stared at the train schedules. Nine months, and he'd learned the numbers, too.

"I guess," she said. "You're right. He might be on that one."

"He might," Pal said.

But he wouldn't. The 6324 was an express. It didn't stop here. It would pass them by in a long, silvery rush. The wind from its passing would make them feel empty inside.

His mother looked at her watch. "How long?" she said.

"Twenty-one minutes."

He waited for her to pick up her phone, to call someone, but she didn't. It lay there in her lap. She considered the tracks and the terminal without its trains, without its people. She looked at Pal and down at her hand, still holding his.

He squeezed her fingers lightly.

She squeezed back, and met his eyes.

It seemed, in the sudden moment of quiet, she might say something.

ACKNOWLEDGMENTS

Grateful acknowledgment is made to the magazines where these stories first appeared:

"Lost-and-Found Girls" first appeared in *Lost and Found in Las Vegas: What the City Hides and What it Reveals, Essays and Stories,* ed. *Scott Dickensheets* (2014). "French for Weakling" won *Iron Horse Literary Review*'s Long Story Contest and was published in *Iron Horse Literary Review Online* in the annual "Trifecta Issue" (June 2015). "I Thought of You" first appeared in *Northwind Magazine* (2013), winner of the *Northwind* Short Story Contest. "Leads" was first published in the 13th Annual *Writer's Digest* Short Short Story Competition Collection (June 2013). "Departures and Arrivals" was first published in *3 Elements Review* (Spring 2014).

ABOUT THE WRITER

DAVID ARMSTRONG is the author of the story collection *Going Anywhere* (Leapfrog Press, 2014), and a novella, *Missives from the Green Campaign* (Omnidawn, 2017). His accolades include the *Mississippi Review* Prize, *Yemassee*'s William Richey Short Fiction award, the New South Writing award, *Jabberwock Review*'s Prize for Fiction, and the *Orison Anthology* Award for Fiction. His stories have appeared in *The Magazine of Fantasy & Science Fiction*, *Narrative Magazine*, *Iron Horse Literary Review*, and numerous other magazines and anthologies. He lives in San Antonio with his wife Melinda and their son Emerson. He is an assistant professor of creative writing in the English Department at the University of the Incarnate Word.